Praise for Savannah Carlisle

". . . Savannah Carlisle is now one of my go-to authors for heartwarming, Kleenex-clutching, feel-good romance!" — **Annie Rains, USA Today bestselling author**

"A charming, inspiring, and empowering second-chance summer romance that will make your heart sing!" — **Karen Schaler, Emmy award-winning screenwriter** on *The Summer of Starting Over*

"Carlisle's novel is thoughtful, with well-developed characters who move beyond common small-town girl and big-city boy tropes. Instead, she pulls together two characters who turn out to have far more in common than they think." — **Kirkus Reviews** on *The Library of Second Chances*

"I was completely enchanted by this charmingly sweet beach read and just adored the letters exchanged in the Little Free Library."— **Teri Wilson, USA Today bestselling author** on *The Library of Second Chances*

"Fans of You've Got Mail will swoon over Lucy and Logan in this charming romance that celebrates the splendor of small-town living." — **KJ Micciche, author of *The Book Proposal*** on *The Library of Second Chances*

". . . Savannah Carlisle's debut is sure to delight. The author's vivid descriptions put me right in Heron Isle along with the characters and had this city girl longing for the cozy and picturesque small-town life she masterfully depicted." — **Meredith Schorr, author of *As Seen on TV* and *Someone Just Like You*** on *The Library of Second Chances*

Also by Savannah Carlisle

The Library of Second Chances
The Summer of Starting Over, Big Dune Island #1
If I'd Have Known, Big Dune Island #2
Finding Me, Finding You (novella)

Christmas at Pine Ridge Inn

SAVANNAH
CARLISLE

To my parents, who always made Christmas magical (and never wrapped my birthday presents in Christmas paper).

One

The infinity pool at Oceanview Resort stretched toward the horizon, its mirrored surface reflecting the mid-December sun. Lila McAllister stood on the terrace above it, tablet in hand, making final notes as she wrapped up her latest consulting gig. Another five-star resort optimized for maximum revenue while also prioritizing guest satisfaction.

"The new check-in system will reduce wait times by thirty percent," she told the manager, Patricia Wu, who nodded approvingly beside her. "And relocating the concierge desk to the lobby's north corner creates better traffic flow and opens up more of those ocean views your guests love."

Patricia smiled. "I don't know why we didn't think of that. We've been struggling with that bottleneck between the front desk and the concierge for months."

Lila shrugged, sliding her tablet into her handbag. "Sometimes all you need is a fresh set of eyes. When you're too close to it, you can't see the obvious solutions." The irony wasn't lost on her that she could solve everyone's problems but her own these days.

"Will you be heading home for the holidays?" Patricia asked as they walked back toward the main building.

"Something like that." Lila forced a smile.

Home wasn't her condo in Huntington Beach with the peekaboo ocean view where she'd return tonight. It was the house where she'd grown up in the suburbs of Atlanta and spent every Christmas of her entire life. Well, every Christmas except the one she was born on and this year.

She hadn't sold the house in Atlanta yet, but she knew she'd have to soon. It wasn't the same now that both of her parents were gone. It would feel just as empty and lonely as her condo, maybe even more so since she knew exactly what it should sound like at Christmastime.

Twenty minutes later, Lila was in her car, heading north on the Pacific Coast Highway through Laguna Beach. The coastline whizzed by, a blurred mix of towering palm trees, red tile roofs, and glimpses of blue ocean between buildings.

Her phone rang through the car speakers, her best friend Jenna's name appearing on the car's LCD screen.

"Hey," Lila answered, already knowing what the call would be about.

"Please tell me you've finally booked your flights for Christmas," Jenna said without bothering to waste time with pleasantries. "The kids have been asking about Aunt Lila all week."

Lila's chest tightened. Jenna had been trying to take care of her since her mother's funeral, inviting her to join her family for Thanksgiving and now Christmas. Lila had the excuse of the job at the Oceanview Resort over Thanksgiving, but she hadn't managed to find one Jenna would accept for Christmas.

Jenna's parents and her in-laws would be there for the holiday, and the last thing they needed was a melancholy houseguest ruining the magic. Not to mention the last thing Lila could stomach this year was being around a happy family to remind her of everything she'd lost. Nope, she was skipping Christmas this year.

"Actually, I might need to take a rain check," Lila said carefully. "Something's come up."

"Work?" Jenna's voice carried a note of concern. "Lila, you've been taking on too many projects. There's a difference between distracting yourself in a healthy way and avoiding dealing with your grief."

"Not work. Personal stuff." Lila paused, choosing her words. "I think I'm finally ready to look into my birth family. It's the first break I've had in months, and I want to spend a little time digging into it and just getting my condo organized. I still have all those boxes I brought home from my parents' house."

The silence stretched for several heartbeats. Jenna knew Lila had been adopted and that Lila's curiosity about her birth parents had grown stronger since she'd lost the parents who'd raised her. Lila's mother had passed back in the spring, just a few short years after her father.

"Oh honey, are you sure? I mean, I think it's wonderful if you're ready to look for your birth mother, but during the holidays? That seems like a lot of emotional weight."

"Maybe that's exactly when I need to do it," Lila said. "Christmas has always felt complicated for me, you know? Being born on Christmas Day and never knowing anything about the circumstances surrounding my birth. Maybe it's finally time to figure that out."

"Do you even know where to start?"

"I have a box of stuff my mom kept. There must be something in there that will give me a clue." Lila stopped at a red light and looked out at the way the sun made the turquoise water of the Pacific sparkle on the surface like glittering diamonds had been strewn across it. "And honestly, Jen, you don't need me there. You've got such a beautiful family Christmas planned. I'd just be the sad single friend bringing down the mood."

"You would not—"

"I would, and we both know it." Lila's voice was gentle but firm. "This year I need to do something different. I promise you I'll be okay. It's what I feel like I need to do right now."

Jenna sighed. "Okay. But keep me updated on what you find. And if you change your mind, just hop on a flight and we'll have a spot ready for you at our table."

"I promise. Give the kids extra hugs from me and tell them I'm mailing their presents."

As she pulled into her parking spot a little over a half hour later, Lila sat in the car for a moment and stared up at the second-story windows of her unit. The apartment had been perfect when she'd moved in three years ago. It was walking distance to the beach and dozens of good restaurants and cute little shops. It was everything she'd thought she wanted, but it still didn't feel like home. Not the way the house she'd grown up in had.

Lila climbed the exterior stairs to her door, keys jingling softly in her hand. Once inside, late afternoon light slanted through the windows, illuminating dust motes that danced above hardwood floors her mother had helped her pick out when she'd bought the place. Everything was exactly as she'd left it that morning—laptop closed on the dining table, coffee mug rinsed and waiting in the sink, throw pillows arranged just so on the sofa.

It somehow looked both lived in and not. Like how you'd set up a photo of a condo to make it look like someone lived there.

Lila dropped her purse by the door, then walked to her bedroom closet. Shoved way in the back was a medium-sized cardboard box she'd taken from her parents' house after her mother's funeral. She'd avoided looking at it for months. Her adoptive parents were her real parents, she felt that to her core. She'd had a wonderful childhood, and they'd been her best friends as an adult. No doubt, that's why she'd never felt the need to know more about her birth parents.

After her mother passed, it felt like a betrayal to suddenly go looking for them. But today felt different. Two weeks away from Christmas—from her birthday—it suddenly felt like the right time. Maybe just as a distraction since she didn't have a new work project to bury herself in, but she didn't want to overanalyze it.

Lila carried the box to her bed and lifted the lid slowly, like something might jump out at her. Inside were the few items that had come with her as a baby. There was a small teddy bear, the pale pink onesie she'd been wearing when her parents picked her up from the agency, and a tiny quilt of red, green, and white squares interspersed with patterned squares in the same colors. Her mother had saved everything for her in case she wanted them some day.

Lila had looked through these things countless times over the years, but today she found herself studying each item more carefully. The teddy bear was well-loved but simple, the kind you could buy at any department store. The onesie had faded from its original pink but showed no identifying marks. The quilt was a little worn around the edges, but the colors were still vibrant and festive.

There had to be something here that could give her a starting point. Some clue that would help her figure out more about where—and who—she came from.

Lila set the items aside and dug deeper into the box. Underneath was a manila folder she'd glanced at before but never thoroughly examined. Inside were official documents from the adoption agency, including the amended birth certificate with her adopted name and adoptive parents' names, and correspondence between the agency and her parents.

She spread the papers across her bed, reading each one carefully. Most of the information was clinical and impersonal, but one document caught her attention: a letter from the adoption counselor to her parents dated three weeks after her birth.

The birth mother has expressed her desire that the child know she was loved and wanted, but that circumstances made it impossible for her to provide the life she hoped her daughter would have. She specifically requested that the quilt and bear accompany the child as reminders that she was cherished from her first moments.

Lila's vision blurred as she read the words again. Her birth mother had wanted her to know she was loved. She'd read the letter once before, but it had been sometime during her teenage years. At the time, she didn't remember that single line making her heart squeeze the way it was now.

But the letter raised more questions than it answered. What circumstances? Was her birth mother young, unmarried, facing family pressure? Or had there been something else—financial hardship, health issues, a relationship that couldn't weather the reality of an unplanned pregnancy?

Lila picked up her phone and scrolled through her contacts until she found the number for Janet Morrison, the attorney who'd handled the estate planning for her parents. Janet specialized in family law and had been her mother's college roommate. Maybe she knew something about navigating adoptions.

"Lila, how wonderful to hear from you," Janet said as she answered.

"I hope I'm not catching you at a bad time."

"Not at all. How are you holding up, honey?"

"I'm managing. Actually, I was hoping you might be able to help me with something. I'm thinking about trying to learn more about my birth family, and I wondered if you could tell me what my options are."

There was a pause. "Of course. Are you thinking about attempting contact, or just trying to get access to information?"

"I'm not sure yet. I guess I'd like to start with information and go from there." She wanted to do an internet search or two on this person before she decided whether it was someone she wanted to contact.

"If I remember correctly, you were born in Colorado, right?"

"Yes." It was one of the few details Lila knew about her birth.

"I'm not well-versed in Colorado law, but I can look into it. Can you give me a couple of days?"

"Of course," Lila said.

After hanging up, Lila carefully gathered the documents and placed them back in the folder. Soon, maybe she'd find out what was actually possible. Maybe the sealed adoption could be opened with the right legal approach. Weren't there databases or registries that could help adoptees connect with their birth families?

A quick internet search revealed that there were indeed registries in some states. In others—like Colorado, apparently—you had to petition the court to get access to your original birth certificate, and then it was only granted if there was a valid reason, like a medical condition. After another half hour of research, she still wasn't clear on exactly what constituted a "valid reason."

Frustrated, Lila tossed the folder on her nightstand and shut her laptop. There was no use in her spinning her wheels trying to research it online. Janet would understand it better than she would.

She'd waited thirty-four years, what was a couple more days?

Two

Three days later, Lila sat at her dining table with her laptop open, waiting for Janet to join their video call. The manila folder lay beside her keyboard, its contents organized and ready to discuss.

Janet's face appeared on screen, her dark hair pulled back in the same neat bun she'd worn for as long as Lila could remember. "Good morning, honey. I've been doing some research since you called."

"Thank you for making time for this." Lila held up the folder. "I have the documents from when I was adopted if you think there's anything useful in here."

"Why don't you tell me what you're hoping to accomplish? Are you looking for medical information, or are you hoping to make contact with your birth family?"

Lila paused, realizing she hadn't fully defined her goals even to herself. "I think I'd like to start with just learning more about the circumstances of my birth. Maybe understanding why my birth mother chose adoption. Then, if that goes well, perhaps I'd be open to contact."

Janet nodded thoughtfully. "Okay, let's start with what's possible in Colorado, since that's where you were born. I have to tell you upfront that Colorado is one of the more restrictive states when it comes to adoption records."

Lila's heart sank, but she tried to stay optimistic. "What does that mean exactly?"

"Adult adoptees in Colorado can only obtain their original birth certificate through a court order, and courts typically require what they consider 'good cause' to grant access. Medical necessity is usually the main qualifying factor."

"What about other records? Anything from the adoption agency?"

"Most adoption agencies are bound by the same confidentiality requirements that sealed your records in the first place. They can't really provide anything that could lead to identification."

The conversation continued for another twenty minutes, with Janet explaining the various databases and search methods available. Most required significant fees with no guarantee of results, and all of them seemed to depend on factors completely outside Lila's control. Then there was always the DNA test route. She could take one and hope her birth mother or another relative had done one too and would show up as a match.

"I'm sorry to be the bearer of disappointing news," Janet said as they wrapped up the call. "I know this isn't what you were hoping to hear. If you do decide to pursue any of these options, I can recommend some reputable search consultants, but I want you to go in with realistic expectations."

After they hung up, Lila stared at her laptop screen, feeling utterly deflated. She'd known it was a long shot, but hearing the legal realities laid out so starkly made her quest feel nearly impossible. Even if she spent thousands of dollars on search consultants and databases, success would depend entirely on whether her birth mother wanted to be found.

Frustrated, Lila closed the laptop and gathered the papers back into the folder. She carried the folder to her bedroom, intending to return it to the box and put this whole idea behind her.

She'd unpacked the box so she could lay the folder at the bottom where it wouldn't get bent, but when she went to place the quilt on top something snagged her eye that she hadn't noticed before. A small fabric label had been sewn in the corner, but it blended in with the pattern of the square. She held it up to the window, squinting at the faded green threads: Made with love by Emily.

Her heart began to beat faster. *Emily*.

Was Emily her birth mother? Had she made her this quilt so Lila could take a piece of her birth mother with her?

No, that would be pretty bold for someone who'd chosen a closed adoption.

But it was still something. One more clue she could add to the short list of things she knew about her birth.

Lila grabbed her phone and took a clear photo of the label with an app that allowed her to search the web by an image. It was a long shot, but she wasn't sure what else to do with the information.

The results appeared almost instantly, and Lila's breath caught. The third result down showed a nearly identical label on a shop's website: Emily's Yarn & Quilts - Pine Ridge, Colorado - Family owned since 1982.

Pine Ridge, Colorado. Lila had never heard of it. She clicked through to the shop's website, studying every photo. The wooden building with cozy storefront windows in the first photo looked warm and inviting. Photos of the inside showed shelves full of colorful yarn, quilts displayed hanging from the walls, and an older woman with kind eyes standing behind the counter—presumably Emily.

Lila opened a new window and searched for Pine Ridge, Colorado. It appeared to be a half hour outside of Breckenridge. A place she'd never been but had at least heard of.

Before she could lose her nerve, Lila switched windows, found the phone number for the store and dialed.

"Emily's Yarn & Quilts, this is Cynthia," a woman's warm voice answered.

"Hi, Cynthia. I'm hoping you might be able to help me," Lila began, her mouth suddenly dry. "I have a quilt that I believe was made in your shop, and I'm trying to learn more about it."

"Oh, how wonderful! Can you describe it?"

Lila did and mentioned the label with Emily's name.

There was a pause. "That would have been my mother's work," Cynthia said, her voice softer now. "She passed away five years ago, but she made so many beautiful pieces over the years. Do you know approximately when it was made?"

"I think around thirty-four years ago. It was made for a baby." Lila paused, debating how much more she wanted to share. "I don't know who bought it though and am trying to find out more about it."

"My mother didn't keep exact records about which quilt was bought by whom, and even if she had I probably wouldn't be able to share it for privacy reasons." Cynthia sounded genuinely apologetic.

"Of course," Lila said quickly, disappointment flooding through her. "I understand."

"Do you live nearby? If you'd like to bring it by the shop, I can tell you more about the pattern and the techniques my mother used," Cynthia offered kindly. "Sometimes seeing the actual piece helps me remember things. I would have worked in the shop back then with my mother, and our quilts weren't sold anywhere else."

"I don't live nearby, but I'm actually thinking about planning a visit soon." It wasn't true, but she'd acted on impulse. "Where exactly are you located?"

"We're right on Main Street in Pine Ridge. It's beautiful here this time of year. I'd definitely suggest visiting if you've never been."

After promising Cynthia she'd stop by if she visited and hanging up, Lila sat on her bed holding the quilt, gripping it in her hand the way a child might for comfort.

Pine Ridge, Colorado. She'd never been to Colorado. You might even say she'd avoided it, like if she ever set foot in the state she'd run into her birth mother, recognize her instantly and devastate the mother who'd raised her by connecting with this other woman.

But someone in Pine Ridge had cared enough to buy a beautiful quilt for a baby girl they'd ultimately given up for adoption. What if that person was still there?

Lila opened her laptop and began researching. Pine Ridge appeared to be a small mountain town with a historic main street that couldn't have been home to more than a dozen businesses. In the photos, it was surrounded by snow-covered peaks. It looked like the kind of place where everyone knew everyone. Maybe the kind of place where secrets were hard to keep.

It appeared there was only one lodging option in town: Pine Ridge Inn. It was a rustic looking bed-and-breakfast with a wraparound porch. The rooms looked comfy, although not the four- or five-star accommodation she generally stayed in for her job as a hospitality consultant. According to the inn's website, they offered special holiday packages for guests wanting a cozy mountain Christmas experience.

Although she had little interest in the holiday this year, it did give her a good excuse to be in town if anyone asked. She could book a stay, explore the town, visit Emily's shop, and maybe find someone who remembered a woman in town who was pregnant thirty-four years ago.

Before she could second-guess herself, Lila clicked through to the inn's reservation page. They had availability starting December twentieth—just three days away. The holiday package included breakfast, dinner, and Christmas activities. It was exactly what someone escaping their regular life for the holidays might choose.

She filled out the reservation form, her fingers trembling slightly as she typed.

Name: Lila McAllister
Number of guests: One
Dates: December 20 to December 24

Three full days in town should give her plenty of time. The only problem was she received an error when she hit the submit button. The holiday package required a stay from December 20th to December 26th.

Fine. She'd book a week but still keep her plan to be back home alone by Christmas Day. The last thing she wanted was forced merriment with strangers.

When she hit submit, her heart hammered against her ribs. She'd done it. In three days, she'd be in Pine Ridge, Colorado, carrying a quilt made by Emily, looking for answers she'd tried not to wonder about her entire life.

Lila carefully folded the quilt and placed it back in the box, along with the other precious few items from her infancy. Outside her windows, the Southern California sun was setting over the pier, painting the sky in shades of pink and gold. Soon she'd be trading palm trees for pine trees.

She wasn't sure what she hoped to find in Pine Ridge, but she felt certain she needed to go.

Three

The GPS in her rental car led Lila through winding mountain roads as afternoon light faded behind heavy clouds. Pine Ridge emerged from the valley like something from a Christmas card—a collection of painted wooden buildings with trim in varying colors, their windows glowing golden in the early evening light. Main Street stretched before her, lined with old-fashioned streetlamps wrapped in evergreen garland and red velvet bows.

Her chest tightened at the sight. The town was straight out of a fairytale, or at least one of those Hallmark movies that played all season long. Had she been here to truly just enjoy the holiday, she might park her car and get out to admire the window displays and breathe in the crisp winter air while sipping a peppermint mocha.

But this year, all that Christmas magic felt like a weight pressing on her lungs. She definitely had to get back home for Christmas so she could mope alone.

She drove slowly past Emily's Yarn & Quilts, a cozy storefront she recognized from its website. In person, she could tell the sign was hand-painted, and someone had taken a lot of time putting together a festive window display. The shop was already closed for the day, but it would be at the top of her to-do list tomorrow.

Pine Ridge Inn sat at the end of Main Street backed up against the mountains. It was a three-story log structure surrounded by a split wood fence. Warm light spilled from the windows, and garland wound around every post and railing. Icicle lights framed the porch, and even the inn's sign was decorated with a small wreath. She'd gone from avoiding Christmas this year to putting herself smack in the middle of a made-for-television Christmas movie.

Lila parked and sat for a moment, gripping her steering wheel. She could do this. She'd stayed in hundreds of hotels for work. This was just another accommodation, another place to sleep while she completed a project.

The walk from the small parking lot up the sidewalk to the inn had been cleared of snow. The building itself appeared to be well taken care of, and the small touches, like a seasonal doormat that read Be Merry and a wreath of fresh fir branches, were welcoming.

When Lila pushed open the front door, she heard the jingle of sleigh bells, and warmth enveloped her immediately. A fire crackled in a stone fireplace surrounded by overstuffed chairs and sofas. Christmas garland draped the mantel, interspersed with white lights that cast everything in a soft glow. The scent of pine and cinnamon hung in the air, along with something that might have been hot cider, making her stomach growl.

"You must be Lila!" A woman in her sixties appeared from behind a rustic front desk, her reddish-blonde hair pulled back in a neat bun and her eyes bright. "I'm Carol

Brennan. We're so glad you chose to spend the holidays with us. You got lucky, you know. We usually book up for Christmas months in advance, but we had a cancellation this year."

"Thank you for having me," Lila managed, forcing a smile. The enthusiasm in Carol's voice made her feel guilty for being there under false pretenses.

"Tom, come meet our guest from California," Carol called toward an open door behind the desk.

A tall man with a graying beard emerged, wiping his hands on a towel. "Welcome to Pine Ridge Inn. I hope the drive wasn't too difficult."

"It was beautiful," Lila said, which was true. The mountains covered in snowy pines had been stunning, even if she'd been too nervous about the windy roads to fully appreciate them.

"We were just setting up for evening refreshments," Carol said, gesturing toward a sideboard that held two urns—one labeled for cider and one for hot cocoa—and a plate of cookies. "Nothing fancy, just a chance for our holiday guests to get acquainted. Most folks are settling into their rooms right now, but you're welcome to grab something hot to drink and warm up by the fire."

Holiday guests. Right. Lila had temporarily forgotten she was part of a package deal. "How many guests are you expecting?"

"Eight, including you," Tom said. "Nice intimate group for the holiday activities. Tomorrow we'll start with snowshoeing, then cookie baking and decorating in the afternoon."

"Friday we'll all go out and pick the tree, then come back to make ornaments and decorate, and then Saturday is the festival downtown," Carol added as she practically buzzed with excitement. "We'll keep you busy all the way through the big dinner and sleigh ride on Christmas Eve, and then we'll all have a lovely Christmas together."

The weight in Lila's chest grew heavier. She'd assumed she could simply avoid whatever activities the inn had planned, but the Brennans' enthusiasm made it clear they were used to everyone participating. "That all sounds lovely," she said carefully. "Though I'm not sure how much I'll be joining in. I'm here more for the quiet retreat aspect."

Carol's expression softened with understanding. "Of course, dear. The holidays can be complicated. All our activities are optional, so you do whatever feels right for you."

Something in her tone suggested she'd hosted guests before who needed space from Christmas cheer. Lila felt a rush of gratitude for the older woman's intuition.

"Also, I know I made my reservation through the twenty-sixth, but I really have to get going on Christmas Eve. I wanted to let you know in case you can book my room for someone else over the holiday."

Carol cheerful expression fell, making her look like a child who'd just learned Santa wasn't real. "You aren't staying for Christmas?"

Lila shook her head. "No, I'm afraid I have other plans."

"Of course, dear. Well, let me show you to your room," Carol said, lifting Lila's suitcase before she could protest. "You're in the Pinecone Room on the second floor. I think you'll love the view."

They climbed a staircase lined with black-and-white photographs of the inn through different decades. "These are wonderful," Lila said, pausing at one that showed the inn in what looked like the 1950s.

"Tom's grandfather built this place in 1923," Carol said proudly. "It's been in the family ever since, though we've made updates over the years to keep guests comfortable."

Lila's consultant eye automatically cataloged details as they walked. The carpet was worn but clean and the fixtures were a bit dated. But something about the inn's cozy feel made her reluctant to mentally redesign it. This place had an authentic charm the luxury resorts she usually worked with sometimes lacked.

"Here we are," Carol said, opening a door halfway down the hall. "The Pinecone Room."

The room was smaller than Lila was used to but undeniably cozy. A queen-sized bed dominated the space, covered with a hand-stitched quilt in shades of cream and forest green. The pattern reminded her immediately of her baby quilt. They weren't identical, but similar enough to make her breath catch. A wingback chair sat by the window, and a small writing desk occupied the corner.

"The bathroom is just through there," Carol said, pointing to a door beside the closet. "And you have a lovely view of Main Street and the mountains beyond."

Lila moved to the window and looked out at the snow-covered rooftops below. In the gathering darkness, every building glowed with warm light, and she could see a few people moving along the sidewalks in their long winter coats and hats.

"It's lovely," she said. "Thank you."

"Dinner is at six-thirty if you'd like to join us," Carol said. "Nothing formal, just a chance for everyone to meet and go over the week's activities. Unfortunately, we only have one restaurant in town open for dinner, so we try our best to make sure no one goes to bed hungry."

After Carol left, Lila sat on the edge of the bed and looked around her temporary home. She unpacked methodically, hanging her clothes in the small closet and arranging her toiletries in the bathroom. The baby quilt she placed carefully on the end of the bed, her fingers drifting over the stitching around the edge.

Tomorrow, she would take the quilt to Emily's Yarn & Quilts and hope that Cynthia remembered something—anything—that might point her toward answers. Tonight, she just had to get through dinner with a group of strangers who were probably thrilled to be spending Christmas in this magical little town. She might have skipped the meal, but she'd already foregone lunch in her efforts to get to Pine Ridge before dark.

As six-thirty approached, Lila made her way downstairs. The dining room was just off the main lobby, decorated with the same Christmas touches as the rest of the inn. There was a single candle in each window and a festive display of garland with little red berries down the middle of the table winding between hurricane lamps that cast a warm glow.

A man was setting up the buffet along one wall, moving between the kitchen and dining room. He was about her age, with dark hair and a slight five o'clock shadow on his face. It was clear he'd done this many times before as she watched him move easily around the room.

Lila's consultant eye automatically assessed the setup. The buffet was positioned in a way that would create a bottleneck when guests lined up to fill their plates. Everything was in one long line instead of separating the salad ingredients, hot food, dessert, and drinks into smaller stations where people could move around out of order. There was plenty of room along the other wall to break the buffet at least in half, and that simple repositioning would improve flow significantly.

"Excuse me," she said, approaching the man. "I couldn't help but notice the serving arrangement. If you moved the beverage station and salad bar to the other wall, it would prevent guests from having to cross paths when they're getting food and drinks. Then you'd also have room here to space out the hot food so those who only want one or the other can skip around instead of waiting in line."

He looked up from arranging silverware, a frown furrowing his brows. "Thanks for the suggestion," he said, "but our guests aren't really in a hurry. They come here to slow down and relax."

There was something in his tone that made it clear he didn't welcome her input. Not rude, exactly, but definitely dismissive. Lila felt heat rise in her cheeks.

"Of course," she said quickly. "I didn't mean to overstep. I work in hospitality, so sometimes I just can't help noticing these things."

"I've worked *here*," he said, emphasizing the word, "for nearly twenty years, so I know how to take care of our guests." Turning his back to her, he continued setting up.

"Lila, I see you've met our manager, Brady Hanson." Carol's voice came from the doorway.

Brady straightened, giving Carol a warm smile that was completely different from the guarded expression he'd worn with Lila. "I'll start setting the table," he said to Carol before turning back to give Lila a once over before retreating into the kitchen.

"Brady's a bit protective of how things are done around here," Carol said gently. "Don't take it personally, dear."

But it felt personal. Lila couldn't shake the feeling that Brady had sized her up in those few minutes and somehow found her lacking. Or maybe he'd simply categorized her as another interfering guest who thought she knew better. She'd certainly encountered that before at other hotels and resorts.

"Is he your son?" Lila asked.

A shadow crossed Carol's face before she quickly replaced it with a tight smile. "No, unfortunately having children wasn't in the cards for me. I'd certainly be proud to have a son like him though."

Other guests began filtering into the dining room, greeting Carol before grabbing drinks and beginning to claim spots at the table. There was an older couple and two women who looked like they could be sisters. Lila spotted a woman alone near the end of the table who looked to be in her mid-fifties. She was reading a book, glasses sliding down her nose as her short brown hair framed her face.

"Mind if I join you?" Lila asked as she approached the empty seat next to the woman.

"Please do," the woman said, closing her book and smiling. "I'm Sarah."

"I'm Lila. Nice to meet you."

"Are you here by yourself?" Sarah asked. She didn't say it with the pity hostesses sometimes used with Lila when she was dining alone. Instead, it sounded like she hoped it was something they had in common.

"I am," Lila said. "How about you?"

"Me too." Sarah's smile was warm. "I've spent a few Christmases here. I guess you could say it's become my Christmas tradition."

"It's my first time here, but it seems like a lovely place to spend the holidays."

"It really is," Sarah said. "Pine Ridge has a way of making you feel less alone."

Lila felt something ease in her chest. Sarah seemed like someone who understood that Christmas wasn't always about unbridled joy and celebration.

Before Lila could ask more questions, Carol, Tom, and Brady began carrying large bowls and platters from the kitchen and encouraged everyone to introduce themselves while they finished getting things set up.

Eight guests were now gathered around a long farmhouse table: Lila and Sarah, an elderly couple from Phoenix, the pair of women who did turn out to be sisters, and a couple closer to Lila's age from Florida. Everyone seemed genuinely excited about the week ahead, discussing the planned activities with enthusiasm that reminded Lila of all the traditions she'd be without this year.

Carol signaled that everyone could line up to fill their plates now, and Lila found herself at the back of the line. Brady was standing off to the side, and Lila noticed how his eyes were scanning the buffet and the guests now lined up waiting for the people in front of them to move forward. Now did he see it the way she had? When his eyes found her at the end of the line, they jumped away as if he hadn't wanted her to catch him looking.

Ha! She was right about the inefficiency of the buffet, and he knew it. That's why he couldn't look at her.

Once everyone was finally seated, Carol, Tom, and Brady grabbed plates and joined them. Carol and Tom clearly enjoyed dining with guests. They answered questions about the planned activities and other things to do in town. Brady took the lead when the question was about outdoor activities like skiing or horseback riding, but it felt more perfunctory than enthusiastic. It was clear the three of them had been doing this for a long time together as they finished each other's sentences and prompted each other to share stories about previous guests.

"So, what brings everyone to Pine Ridge for Christmas?" asked one of the sisters, a cheerful woman named Kimberly.

The answers varied. The older couple, Sophie and Miles, were here to celebrate their fifty-fifth wedding anniversary. They'd spent two nights here after their wedding and always returned for big anniversaries and in years where their daughters both spent their holiday with in-laws. The sisters, Kimberly and Kendall, had come a few times as children and decided to return on their own when their parents booked a Christmas cruise to celebrate their retirement. The younger couple, Ali and Mike, wanted an escape from big city life in Miami and planned to ski a couple of days over in Breckenridge. Sarah, like she'd told Lila, had made her Christmas visits to Pine Ridge Inn a bit of a tradition over the years. When the attention turned to Lila, she felt all eyes on her.

"I needed a change of scenery," she said simply. "This seemed like the kind of place where you could have a quiet, peaceful Christmas."

"Oh, it's anything but quiet," laughed Sophie. "Carol and Tom keep us busy with activities, and the whole town gets involved. There's Christmas caroling, a tree lighting ceremony, and even a Christmas service at the church that's absolutely beautiful."

Lila's chest tightened again. All around the table, the other guests smiled and expressed their delight in being part of this Christmas wonderland. Meanwhile, Lila just wanted to forget it was Christmas and focus on the mission that had brought her here.

"Of course, you can participate as much or as little as you like," Carol said gently, as if sensing Lila's panic. "Some guests prefer simply reading a book by the fire or soaking in the hot tub out back."

"The tree selection is really something special," Sarah said, turning to Lila. "Brady takes us up into the woods where the Brennans have permission to cut, and we help choose the inn's Christmas tree."

"And then we make ornaments and decorate it together," Carol added. "I must admit, it's my favorite of our holiday activities."

"I might sit that one out," Lila said. "I'm not much for the outdoors in winter."

Sarah caught her eye and gave her a small, understanding smile. Not judgment, just recognition that it might be too much for her.

"The cookie baking is indoors," Carol offered. "And you get first dibs on anything you bake."

"Maybe," Lila said noncommittally.

"Brady has offered to help us set up luminaries along the fence and down the drive too," said Kendall. "We're from Santa Fe, and it's a big part of the Christmas tradition there that we hate to miss."

Lila glanced at Brady, who was refilling water glasses at the other end of the table. His investment in the holiday experience for the guests was obvious, but he wasn't exactly giving out the warm fuzzy vibes to match. He was handsome, that was hard not to notice with his tall, strong build and angular jaw. But he was a quiet man who seemed focused on just doing his job.

The conversation moved on to other topics—the weather forecast, recommendations for exploring the town, stories about Pine Ridge's colorful history. Lila found herself listening carefully for anything that might aid in her investigation, but she simply didn't have enough to go on yet. Hopefully, the visit to the yarn store would help.

After dinner, she excused herself and retreated to her room. The inn had grown quiet, other guests settling in for the night or gathering around the fireplace downstairs. Out her bedroom window, she noticed Brady standing at the fence where it appeared a section of the Christmas lights had gone dark. They really should change over to the strands that stay lit even when one bulb goes out. He would probably be about as receptive to that as the buffet suggestion though.

Lila sat in the wingback chair and looked past Brady down Main Street. A few people moved along the sidewalks, the warm light of the streetlamps illuminating them. Somewhere in this small town, could there be someone who remembered a pregnant woman from thirty-four years ago? Had she lived here or just been passing through when she bought the quilt?

The quilt sat on the end of the bed like a question waiting to be answered. Tomorrow, she would take it to

Emily's Yarn & Quilts and hope that Cynthia might know something useful. Tonight, she just had to figure out how to navigate the coming days of Christmas activities she had no interest in joining without being rude to her hosts, who seemed like lovely people.

Outside her window, Brady's silhouette moved up the drive toward the porch, and he appeared to glance up at her window, like he felt her eyes on him. Embarrassed, she pulled the curtains closed and began preparing for bed.

Lila was scared about what she might learn tomorrow. She was even more scared, however, of the chance that she might learn nothing at all. For the first time in her life, she felt like she needed to know where she came from, and Pine Ridge was beginning to feel like a nice place to have roots.

Four

Lila pulled back the curtains the next morning to find Main Street covered in a fresh blanket of white as the early morning light began to illuminate it. Fat flakes continued to drift down, transforming the town into a scene from a snow globe. She'd seen snow before during business trips to places like Tahoe and Park City, but in those instances, it was always an element to be dealt with, not a postcard-perfect picture to enjoy.

For a moment, she let herself appreciate the beauty of it. Then she remembered why she was here, and the familiar weight settled back into her chest.

Downstairs, the inn was still quiet. It was early, and breakfast wouldn't be served for another hour and a half, but Carol had shown her a small nook on her floor with a couple of chairs and a coffee machine that made one cup at a time. In desperate need of her morning ritual, Lila padded down the hall in her pajamas and a robe hoping it was early enough to avoid running into anyone else.

However, she arrived to find one of the two chairs in the nook already occupied by Sarah, her hands wrapped around a steaming mug.

"Good morning," Sarah said, smiling up at her. "You're an early riser too?"

More like a poor sleeper, but Lila forced a smile. "Nothing a little coffee can't fix."

As she was waiting for the machine to brew her cup, Lila turned to look out the picture window Sarah was facing. The yard stretched out behind the inn for two hundred yards or more before it hit a mountainside, snow-covered pines dotting the landscape. There were two cabins in the distance, just at the tree line.

"Are those part of the inn too?" Lila asked. There was no separate driveway to them, only a path that had been partially covered by the snow, so she wondered if that was where Carol and Tom lived.

Sarah nodded. "One is Carol and Tom's, and the other is Brady's. I don't think they spend much time there other than to sleep though."

"Brady lives on the property too?" Lila was surprised. It made sense that the Brennans lived there, as most B&B owners lived on their properties. Brady must receive housing as part of his compensation package.

"Since he was a teenager," Sarah said. "Carol and Tom took him in after his parents were killed in a car crash. I was here that first Christmas afterward and heard all about how the whole town came together for him. It's a special place."

That really did sound awful to have lost his parents at the same time before he was even an adult.

"Wow, you really have been coming here a long time," Lila said, not sure what else to say. It felt weird knowing something so personal about a man who'd basically dismissed her earlier.

"I love Pine Ridge at Christmas," Sarah said, not offering any additional explanation for her frequent visits.

Lila's coffee finished brewing and she grabbed the warm mug, planning to take it back to her room. Before she could tell Sarah she'd see her later, the woman patted the arm of the chair next to her. "Come sit." Sarah pointed out the window. "We have visitors this morning."

Turning to look, Lila saw a doe and a smaller deer tiptoeing out of the tree line and onto the field between the cabins. She settled into the chair, cupping her mug with her hands. The deer moved gracefully through the snow, their breath visible as small puffs in the cold morning air.

"One of the benefits of being an early riser," Sarah said softly. "I've seen moose and elk here too. I love having my first cup of coffee here every morning during my stay. Such a peaceful way to start the day."

"It's a beautiful spot," Lila agreed.

The larger doe lifted her head, alert, then seemed to decide all was well and returned to chewing on some kind of brush. The smaller deer stayed close to her side.

"A mother and her child," Sarah observed quietly.

Lila felt an unexpected tightness in her chest, unable to reply. She missed her mother so much it physically hurt in moments like this, and yet watching the two graceful animals reminded her of all the beautiful things still left in the world

The women sat quietly, sipping their coffee while the deer moved around the brush and nibbled. It was nice to be able to sit with someone and not have to keep up a conversation while enjoying something as simple as watching wildlife out the window.

"Well," Sarah said, standing as the deer began to wander back toward the trees, "I should let you enjoy your morning in peace. Thank you for sharing the view with me."

"Thank you for pointing them out," Lila said. "I probably would have missed them entirely."

Sarah smiled. "That's what Pine Ridge is for . . . slowing down to appreciate the little things."

After Sarah left, Lila remained in the chair, watching the empty field where the deer had been. She had come to town for something else entirely, but it didn't hurt to enjoy the scenery while she was there.

Freshly showered and dressed an hour later, Lila heard the others stirring downstairs as her stomach growled for breakfast. As she made her way down and into the lobby though, she didn't see anyone else yet.

As she approached the dining room, she heard a mechanical whirring followed by what sounded like disgruntled mumbling.

She found Brady crouching over the coffee station in the dining room, tools spread around him as he worked on what appeared to be an ancient coffee machine. A panel was removed, revealing a tangle of wires and components that looked like a science experiment gone wrong.

Brady glanced up. "The machine's acting up, but there's a single-serve unit upstairs if you don't want to wait." He returned his attention to the machine, adjusting something with his screwdriver.

Lila moved closer, studying the ancient contraption. "You know, there are some fantastic commercial-grade machines I always recommend to my clients. The Brew Pro 11 is what most of the high-end hotels use. It can handle high volume and makes perfect espressos, cappuccinos, and lattes. It really elevates the guest experience."

Brady paused in his work and looked up at her with the same frown of disappointment he'd given her the previous evening. "This machine makes coffee just fine when it's working properly. Our guests don't need dessert masquerading as coffee. They come here for the simple and traditional, not fancy and over the top."

"I just meant—"

"This isn't the kind of town that needs a Starbucks on the corner," Brady snarked.

Heat crept up Lila's neck. She'd only been trying to help, but clearly her suggestion wasn't welcome. "Of course. I didn't mean to imply there was anything wrong with how you do things. Just trying to make your job a little easier."

Brady's expression softened slightly, as if he realized he'd been sharper than necessary. "Thanks, but I'm good."

Remembering what Sarah had told her that morning about his parents, Lila cut him some slack and backed away to find a seat at the table. This probably wasn't his favorite time of year, so she couldn't blame him for being a little prickly.

Carol appeared from the kitchen carrying a tray of pastries as Lila settled in the same chair she'd occupied the night before.

"Can it be resuscitated?" Carol asked Brady.

"Should have it running in a few minutes," Brady said, returning to his work.

"Brady keeps that machine and everything else here running," Carol told Lila with obvious affection. "I don't know what we would do without him." She leaned in conspiratorially. "Don't tell Tom I said this, but he's not very handy with mechanical things."

"Hey, I heard that," Tom said, coming out of the kitchen with a platter full of bacon.

"Love you, honey," Carol said, turning to smile at him.

"She's right," Tom whispered loud enough for Carol to hear as he passed by Lila to place the bacon on the buffet table. "I can build new cabinets and repair the deck, but I stay away from things with wires and plugs."

"You can't be good at everything, darling," Carol assured him as she took the platter from his hands.

Brady was focused intently on the coffee machine, but Lila caught the way a smile played at the corners of his lips as he shook his head at Carol and Tom's playful teasing.

The other guests began filtering in. The older couple, Sophie and Miles, were debating whether to attempt a walk into town given the snow that had fallen overnight or stay in to play cards. Meanwhile, the sisters were excited about the fresh powder for the afternoon's planned activities.

"Are you joining us for snow shoeing?" asked Sarah as she took the seat beside Lila.

"I think I might explore the town a bit instead," Lila said. "Get my bearings."

"Smart choice on a day like this," Sarah said, glancing toward the windows. "The shops on Main Street are lovely, and you can duck inside if the snow gets too heavy."

An hour later, bundled in her warmest coat, Lila stepped out into the falling snow, clutching the quilt under her arm. The cold bit at her cheeks, but it was only a short walk into town. Brady had gone out to shovel the walk from the inn to the street, and the sidewalk into town had already been cleared as well.

In the first block of businesses, Lila passed a bakery with steamed windows and the rich scent of fresh bread, a bookstore with displays of holiday novels, and a small general store. Everyone she encountered smiled and nodded, the kind of friendly acknowledgment that didn't always exist in larger cities.

Emily's Yarn & Quilts sat halfway down the block, its hand-painted sign dusted with snow. Through the windows, Lila could see colorful displays of yarn, fabric, and quilts hanging on the walls like works of art. Her heart beat faster as she pushed open the door.

A bell chimed softly, and a woman emerged from behind a display of holiday-themed fabric. She was perhaps sixty, with silver-streaked brown hair pulled back in a loose bun and kind eyes behind black-rimmed glasses.

"Welcome," the woman said. "Is there anything I can help you find?"

"Are you Cynthia? I called the other day about a quilt I believe came from your store."

"I am, and you must be Lila! I've been hoping you'd stop by this week."

"It's so nice to meet you in person," Lila said, feeling some of her nervousness ease at Cynthia's warm welcome.

"I have to admit, I've been thinking about your quilt ever since you called." Cynthia moved closer, her expression thoughtful. "My mother was very particular about her baby quilts. She always said they carried extra love since they were meant to comfort little ones. They usually included some little touches that were specific to each individual child."

Lila perked up. Was there something on the quilt that might unlock more information about her past? "I know it's a long shot, but do you think you might remember anything about this particular one?" Lila held the quilt out to Cynthia.

"I wish I could say yes, but that was so long ago, and my mother made so many beautiful pieces." Cynthia's eyes were kind but apologetic. "But she did keep journals of her work, especially the commissioned pieces and special orders. I haven't looked through them in years, but if you could leave the quilt with me for a few days, I can take a look. You said you know what year it was made? That would help me find the right journal."

Lila felt a flutter of hope mixed with nervousness. "I believe it would have been made in 1991 because the baby was born Christmas Day that year."

"Oh, a Christmas baby. How wonderful." Cynthia shot Lila a knowing smile. "Was that baby you, by chance?"

Lila hadn't planned on telling Cynthia her whole life story, but maybe some details would help her find the right journal entries. "Yes, so you're probably wondering why I don't know more about it. I was adopted." Cynthia's eyebrows rose in surprise. "I've always known I was born in Colorado, but the quilt is the only other clue I have about my birth. It was a closed adoption, but the quilt was sent with me by my birth mother."

"Oh my," Cynthia said, clutching a hand over her heart as tears gleamed in her eyes. "It seems this quilt is indeed a special one. I'm not sure if I'll find anything, or what would even be appropriate to pass along to you, but I'd be happy to take a look, and we can cross that bridge when we get there."

"Thank you. I really would appreciate anything you can tell me. Even a small detail might help."

"Of course, dear." Cynthia's smile was encouraging. "My mother always believed that quilts had their own stories to tell. Maybe yours is ready to share its story."

Hope fluttered in Lila's chest. "That would be incredible. Thank you."

"It's my pleasure. It's one of the most human things in the world to want to know more about where you came from." She patted the quilt like it was a precious treasure she'd keep safe while in her possession. "How long will you be in town?"

"Until Christmas Eve. I'm staying at Pine Ridge Inn."

"You're not staying for Christmas? Tom and Carol might as well be Mr. and Mrs. Claus for the production they make out of the holiday season."

Lila didn't want to reveal she was opting to spend Christmas alone. "No, I need to get back home." It wasn't a lie. She did need to get back home, lest she ruin Christmas for everyone with her moping.

Cynthia promised to start looking through the journals that evening, and Lila left her cell phone number. Buoyed by the possibility that she might be one step closer, Lila stopped to browse in a couple of the other stores on Main Street, buying a candle holder made from an aspen tree for Jenna and an engraved cutting board for her neighbor, Mrs. Marbry, who always kept an eye on her condo while she was away.

Lila headed back to the inn feeling lighter than she had since arriving in Pine Ridge. Soon, she might finally have some concrete information about where she came from.

Five

Back at the inn, Lila found the lobby empty except for the soft crackling of the fire. The snowshoeing group hadn't returned yet, and the inn was eerily quiet in their absence. She settled into one of the armchairs with a book but found herself watching the snow fall instead of reading.

"How was your exploration?"

Lila looked up to find Carol coming from the kitchen carrying a basket over to the small table along the wall that had held drinks and sweet treats the evening before, when Lila arrived.

"It was lovely. The town is so charming, especially in the snow."

"Did you find what you were looking for?"

Her breath caught in her throat that Carol might have somehow intuited that Lila had come to Pine Ridge searching for something. That was ridiculous, of course. She surely meant a souvenir or perhaps a gift for someone else.

"I bought a couple of gifts for friends at Birchwood's, and I stopped in the quilt and yarn store. All the shops are so cute."

"Oh, you must have met Cynthia at Emily's then. We've been friends since I first moved to town."

"I did," Lila said, deciding not to mention the quilt that brought her to town. "You don't see many shops like that anymore."

Carol nodded, settling into the chair across from her. "Emily was something special. She taught half the town to sew and knit, and her quilts were legendary. She made the ones we keep on the beds in the winter, but when someone had a baby or got married, Emily went all out to mark the occasion." Carol's expression grew fond. "Emily believed in celebrating life's important moments with something made by hand that would last."

Before Lila could respond, the front door burst open with a gust of cold air and laughter. The snowshoeing group had returned, their cheeks red from the cold and their eyes bright with excitement. Brady followed behind, brushing snow from his coat before he came through the front door.

"We had so much fun," Kimberly said.

"And we managed not to get completely lost in the snow," added Kendall with a grin.

"I haven't lost anyone yet," Brady joked as he shrugged off his coat and hung it on a peg by the door.

He certainly seemed to be in a better mood after some time outdoors. Maybe he had hit it off with Kimberly or Kendall? They'd both said the evening before that they were single, and they looked to be in their thirties like Brady.

"Thank goodness. That would be bad for business." Carol laughed. "Brady, would you mind putting a few more logs on the fire while I grab the hot cocoa?"

Brady moved to the fireplace in front of where Lila sat, and she noticed how his green and black plaid flannel shirt brought out the green in his eyes. The shirt tugged tight over his broad shoulders as he leaned over to pick up logs, and she allowed herself to take a longer look at him. He was inarguably attractive with his strong build, angular jaw, and hair that always seemed perfectly swept back. Lila hadn't been on a date since her mother passed, and it was the first time she'd even stopped long enough to notice a handsome man. Of course, he was literally right in front of her, so he was hard to miss.

Sarah came to sit by Lila as the rest of the group dispersed to shower and change clothes. "How was your morning?" she asked.

"I had a nice time shopping downtown."

"She hit Birchwood's and Emily's," Carol supplied as she reentered the room with the carafe of hot chocolate.

"Oh, wonderful," Sarah said. "I always stop by Emily's when I'm in town. There's something soothing about being surrounded by all those cozy quilts. My grandmother loved to sew quilts, so I guess it reminds me of her."

"Do you sew?"

Sarah smiled, but it seemed wistful. "I used to, but it's one of those things that kind of fell out of vogue. Sometimes I think about taking it up again. There's something to be said for creating something beautiful with your hands."

"Speaking of creating things with your hands, I could use some help setting up for cookie decorating if anyone is interested," Carol said. Brady had already exited out the back door, leaving only Lila and Sarah in the lobby.

"I need to grab a quick shower," Sarah said, "but I can help as soon as I get back down."

Carol looked expectantly at Lila, and she found it hard to say no even though she had no plans to participate. She really had no excuse, and it seemed impolite to refuse.

As they worked together in the inn's kitchen a few minutes later, measuring flour and arranging baking sheets, Lila found herself appreciating the way the task kept her mind busy and allowed her to think about something other than the quilt and her potential connection to Pine Ridge.

Carol watched Lila efficiently organize ingredients. "Do you bake much at home?"

"Not really. I'm usually too busy with work to cook much of anything." An image of decorating cookies in the shape of snowmen and reindeer alongside her mother the previous Christmas for the neighborhood cookie swap threatened to take Lila's breath away, but she pushed it aside to revisit later when she was alone.

"What kind of work do you do?"

"I'm a hospitality consultant. I help luxury hotels and resorts improve their operations."

"Oh, boy," Carol said. "I hope we've passed your tests."

Lila laughed, holding her hands up. "No tests. I'm taking a much-needed break from work this week."

"That must be interesting work. Traveling to different places and seeing how they do things."

"It is. Though sometimes I think I've stayed in so many hotels that I've forgotten what home actually feels like."

The admission surprised Lila. She hadn't meant to reveal anything so personal, but something about Carol's gentle presence made her want to share.

"Home isn't always one specific place," Carol said softly. "Sometimes it's a feeling. A simple sense of belonging when you're around people who matter to you."

Before Lila could respond, the kitchen filled with voices as the other guests arrived, some with hair still damp from showers. The space that had felt intimate only moments before was now filled with activity.

"I see we're all ready to go," said Sophie, rolling up her sleeves. "Miles, find me an apron before I get flour all over this sweater."

"I call dibs on the mixer," announced Kimberly, making a beeline for the stand mixer on the counter.

"You always get the mixer," protested her sister. "It's my turn."

"Ladies, ladies," Tom intervened with mock seriousness, "we have multiple mixing bowls. No need for a cookie war."

Lila found herself swept into the cheerful chaos as Carol assigned tasks. Ali and Mike took charge of measuring dry ingredients while debating whether their Miami apartment had enough counter space for serious baking. The sisters stationed themselves at opposite ends of the island, each claiming their own territory for what was clearly a long-standing sibling rivalry.

"Sarah, would you mind helping Lila with the sugar cookies?" Carol asked. "She's got excellent organizational skills." She winked at Lila.

Sarah appeared at Lila's elbow with a gentle smile. "I promise not to mess up your system," she said quietly.

"I'm not sure it's a system so much as controlled chaos at this point." Lila laughed.

They worked side by side, Sarah's steady presence a calming influence as Lila tried to keep track of multiple cookie batches. Sarah had a way of anticipating what was needed, handing Lila ingredients before she even asked. They fell into an easy rhythm while the others buzzed around them.

"Do you bake much at home?" Lila asked. "You seem like you know what you're doing."

"My grandmother taught me when I was little. She always said that baking is like an edible love letter." Sarah's voice carried a note of wistfulness. "I don't bake much anymore, but being in a kitchen like this brings back some really lovely memories."

Across the island, Kimberly had managed to get flour not just in her bowl but somehow in her hair and across her cheek. "How does this even happen?" She laughed, trying to brush the white powder from her face but only succeeding in adding more.

"It's a gift," her sister teased. "Remember when you tried to make Dad's birthday cake, and it looked like a flour bomb had gone off?"

"That cake was delicious, thank you very much."

"The parts that weren't crunchy from the eggshells you left in," her sister shot back.

Their playful banter filled the kitchen with laughter, and Lila found herself smiling as she worked. Maybe taking part in some of the inn's Christmas activities wouldn't be as painful as she'd anticipated. Sure, baking made her think back on the many Christmases she spent in the kitchen baking with her mother, but Lila was surprised to find she felt closer to her as she worked alongside the others instead of saddened by her absence.

Brady appeared in the doorway, surveying the scene with amusement. "How's it going in here? I can hear the laughter from the lobby."

"We're making excellent progress," Carol said, "though I think we're using twice as much flour as necessary."

"That's because Kimberly keeps flinging it around," accused her sister.

"I do not fling. I'm just . . . enthusiastic."

"Need any help?" Brady asked, as he came closer to inspect Sophie's first batch of cookies that had just come from the oven. "I make an excellent taste-testing assistant."

"Absolutely not," Carol said firmly. "You'll eat half of them before we can even get them decorated."

"She's right," Tom agreed, appearing behind Brady. "Remember last year when half the gingerbread men mysteriously lost their heads?"

"That was clearly a cookie emergency," Brady said solemnly. "They were suffering. I put them out of their misery."

The easy teasing between Brady and the Brennans reminded Lila of the dynamic she'd had with her own parents, and the familiar tidal wave of sadness threatened to topple her. Sarah nudged her then, bringing her back to the present.

"Could you grab that cookie sheet from the oven? I think they're done." The knowing look on her face said she sensed Lila needed to keep busy.

As Lila pulled the golden cookies in the shape of snowmen and reindeer from the oven, the warm scent of vanilla and butter filled the air. Steam rose from the hot cookies, and she felt an unexpected sense of accomplishment at the perfectly golden results.

"Those look professional," Ali said admiringly. "You sure you don't bake regularly?"

"I guess it's like riding a bike," Lila said, but she couldn't hide her pleased smile.

As the afternoon progressed, Lila found herself relaxing in ways she hadn't expected. When the sisters' playful argument escalated into an actual flour fight, she surprised herself by laughing instead of stepping back. When Sophie asked her to help with the dough for the gingerbread men, she abandoned her precise measuring approach and went with the older woman's "eyeballing it" method.

"My grandmother always said you could tell if someone was good at baking by how they handled cookie dough," Sophie said, watching Lila work. "Too dry and they'll fall apart. Too wet and they'll wind up spreading too much and flattening into a pancake. You've got it just right though."

The compliment warmed Lila more than it should have. She'd spent years perfecting her professional skills, earning praise for her strategic thinking and efficiency. But when was the last time someone had complimented her on anything but work?

Brady returned as they were transferring the final batches to cooling racks, the kitchen now warm and fragrant with the smell of fresh-baked cookies. Flour dusted every surface, and most of the bakers bore evidence of their afternoon's work on their clothes and hands.

"The lobby smells incredible," he said, stealing a cookie from a cooling rack despite Sophie's protests. "I've got stations all set up for the decorating portion."

"Perfect timing," Carol said, surveying their bounty. "We've got enough cookies to feed the whole town."

As they began carrying platters of cookies to the dining room, Lila realized she'd completely lost track of time. The afternoon had slipped away in a haze of flour and laughter, and for the first time since arriving in Pine Ridge, she hadn't thought about her mission to find her birth mother.

"You coming to decorate?" Kimberly asked, balancing a tray of sugar cookies.

Lila hesitated. She'd planned to retreat to her room to call Jenna or catch up on emails. But looking around at the group that had somehow become familiar in just a few hours, she found herself nodding.

"I wouldn't miss it."

"Excellent," said Sarah with a warm smile. "I wouldn't want to lose my partner."

It was then that Lila remembered she wasn't the only one here alone for the holiday. She didn't know why Sarah wasn't spending the holidays with friends or family, but it warmed her heart that Sarah thought of them as a team. They moved into the dining room where Brady had set up decorating stations with colored icing and sprinkles, and for the first time in months, Lila was looking forward to something that had nothing to do with work.

That evening, after a delicious dinner and a rowdy game of charades in the lobby, Lila retired to her room to take a shower. She was too restless to sleep though, as thoughts of the quilt, and who'd commissioned it, filled her mind. The day's activities had been a welcome distraction, but now in the quiet of her room, all her questions came rushing back. She decided to take her book down to read by the fire for a while, hoping the peaceful atmosphere might calm her racing thoughts.

She was surprised to find Brady in the lobby kneeling beside one of the side tables near the fireplace, tools spread around him as he worked underneath it with careful concentration.

"You're here late," she observed.

He looked up, a screwdriver in his hand. "Just tightening up this table. The legs get loose over time with all the use, and it was starting to wobble when guests set their drinks down."

"Do you mind if I sit? I can be quiet."

Brady studied her for a moment, as if weighing whether he wanted company. "Sure," he finally said.

"Thanks," she said, selecting the same chair she'd sat in earlier that day when she'd talked with Carol.

Brady moved to the fireplace to put more logs on the fire, and Lila found herself studying the lobby with fresh eyes in the soft lamplight. The furniture was arranged in conversation groupings, but there was something about the flow that seemed off to her.

"You know," she said as Brady poked at the logs, "if you moved those two chairs from the corner over here by the fireplace, and shifted that side table to the other wall, you'd create a much better conversation area. The way it's set up now, people sitting over there feel isolated from the main seating area."

Brady returned the tool to its rack by the hearth, turning from the fire to look at her, his expression unreadable. "You said you're a hospitality consultant?"

She nodded. "I go into hotels and resorts and help them improve the guest experience and optimize revenue opportunities."

"And they pay you to tell them how to rearrange their lobby? Or their buffet line?" He looked mildly amused now. Not like he was belittling her profession but like they shared an inside joke.

"Sometimes pool furniture too." She shrugged, smiling.

The joke broke his poker face, and he returned her smile. "Well, thank goodness we don't have a pool."

"Although I did notice that the hot tub . . ." Lila let her voice trail off. She was only joking. She didn't actually have any suggestions for the hot tub she'd seen out the back windows.

Brady shook his head as he laughed. "Yeah, pretty sure even you can't rearrange the hot tub."

"But we *could* rearrange the lobby," she teased, motioning around.

He glanced around as if considering her suggestion. "The furniture has been arranged like this for as long as I can remember."

"I'm sure it has," Lila said, trying not to sound too snarky. It was the first thing people always said when she suggested changes. All joking aside, he'd been pretty prickly about her earlier suggestions, so she tried to tread carefully. After all, no one had hired her to improve this inn. "I didn't mean there was anything wrong with it. It's just that in my work, I notice things like traffic flow, sight lines, and how spaces make people feel."

Brady sat on the hearth, his green eyes studying her face. "Can I ask you something?"

She nodded, bracing herself for another polite but firm dismissal of her suggestions.

"Why do you feel like you need to constantly fix everything?"

The question caught her off guard. It wasn't asked with irritation or judgment, but with genuine curiosity. "I don't need to constantly fix everything," she said defensively.

"Since you've been here, you've suggested improvements to our buffet setup, our coffee machine, and now our furniture arrangement." Brady's tone was direct but had a hint of amusement. "I'm genuinely curious. What drives that?"

Lila felt heat creep up her neck. When he laid it out like that, it did sound excessive. "It's what I'm good at. I see inefficiencies, and I want to help."

"But is it really about helping, or is it about something else?"

She stared at him, taken aback by the perceptiveness of the question. "What do you mean?"

"Sometimes people try to fix everything around them when they can't fix what's bothering them on the inside."

The words hit closer to home than Lila cared to admit. She looked away from his steady gaze, focusing instead on a painting that hung on the wall behind him. It was a watercolor of the inn in summer, surrounded by wildflowers and green mountains under a brilliant blue sky. The brushwork was delicate and expressive, capturing not just the visual details but somehow the feeling of the place.

"That's beautiful," she said pointing at the painting to force a change of subject. "I bet this place is beautiful in the summer."

Brady turned to follow her gaze, and his expression softened. "My mother painted that."

She remembered what Sarah had said about his parents but didn't want to make him uncomfortable that they'd been talking about something so personal. "Clearly a talented lady," Lila said, studying the delicate brushwork more closely.

"She was." He said it matter-of-factly. "She's been gone for a long time now though." He didn't meet her eyes or elaborate.

Lila didn't want to pry, but at least they finally had something they could connect over. "I'm sorry. I lost my mother recently too. It changes everything, doesn't it?"

Brady looked at her for a moment as if sizing up whether he could trust her with his answer. "Yeah, it does." For a moment, he looked like he might say more, but then he stood. "I should let you get back to your book. I need to get some sleep. Early morning tomorrow with the tree hunt."

"Of course," Lila said. "Thanks for letting me sit with you."

He nodded, then gathered his tools and headed toward the back door. She watched the flames dancing in front of her, mesmerized by their movement. For a brief moment, she'd been comforted by the idea that someone else understood what it was like to lose your mother. None of her close friends had been through it. So, she often felt like she had no one to talk to about the times she picked up the phone to call her mother before realizing she wouldn't answer.

The lobby felt especially quiet now that Brady was gone, leaving her alone with her thoughts and the crackling fire. Finding her birth mother wasn't going to fill the hole in her heart. Her mother couldn't be replaced. But she couldn't help hoping that finding her birth mother would heal another wound she'd had—and ignored—for far longer.

Six

For someone who'd wanted nothing more than to spend the holiday season alone just a few days ago, even Lila was surprised by how comforted she was to find Sarah in the upstairs sitting room drinking her coffee the next morning.

"Good morning," Sarah said.

"Morning," Lila said, making her way to the coffee maker. "Have our deer friends arrived yet this morning?"

Sarah shook her head. "Not yet, but I'm hoping to see them again too."

While her coffee brewed, they chatted about the previous evening's game of charades and how hilarious Tom had been trying to act out the Grinch. He'd looked more like a bear attacking a campsite at first, but Ali had finally guessed it when he made a heart with his hands and showed it growing twice in size.

"Are you joining us for the tree hunt today?" Sarah asked as Lila settled in next to her.

"No, I think I'll sit this one out," Lila said as she scanned the tree line for the deer. "I'm not much for hiking around in the snow."

"It's so much fun looking for the right tree that you forget how cold it is," Sarah assured her. "People tend to get a little competitive as they try to be the first to spot the perfect one."

"I bet," Lila said. "I didn't really plan on joining in any of the holiday activities this trip. The cookies were fun yesterday, but I think I might just do some quiet reading today."

Sarah reached over to pat Lila's arm. "I don't know what your story is—and you don't have to tell me—but I understand how difficult the holidays can be. I lost someone I loved right around Christmas a long time ago, but it was actually this place that helped me heal."

Lila's chest tightened. "I'm sorry for your loss."

"It was a long time ago but thank you." Sarah sipped her coffee, her eyes distant. "I spent several Christmases hiding away, trying to pretend the holiday didn't exist. But I learned that sometimes the best way through grief is to let yourself be part of something larger than your sadness."

The words hit closer to home than Lila cared to admit. "Did it help?"

"Eventually. Not right away, but gradually." Sarah's smile was soft. "There's something about being in the woods on a crisp winter morning, breathing fresh air and working with other people toward a common goal. It reminds you that life continues and that there's still beauty to be found."

Lila found herself reconsidering. She'd come to Pine Ridge for answers about her past, but maybe Sarah was right about needing to be part of something larger than her search. Her parents had always bought their tree from their local plant nursery, so it wasn't like she had any memories that would be dredged up on this trek into the woods for a tree. Besides, there wasn't anything she could do until she heard back from Cynthia anyway.

"You know what, you're right," Lila said. "Maybe some fresh air would be nice."

Two hours later, after a big breakfast with the group, everyone gathered on the front porch. Lila was bundled in her warmest coat and the hiking boots she'd thrown into her suitcase at the last minute. Brady was explaining the plan, his breath visible in the cold air as he pointed toward the wooded area behind the inn.

"The Hendersons, who own the land, have given us permission to cut a tree from the designated area," he was saying. "It's about a fifteen-minute walk through some beautiful terrain. Nothing too difficult, and we can stop as often as we need to."

Lila studied the group assembled around Brady. Eight guests, plus Carol, Tom, and Brady, made eleven people to coordinate through the woods. Her consultant mind immediately began calculating logistics.

"Would it make more sense to split into smaller groups?" she asked. "We could cover different quadrants of the area so we can find the tree much faster."

"We could do that," Brady said in a tone that indicated he wasn't considering it as a viable option, "but half the fun is wandering together as a group, discovering trees, debating their merits. It's about the journey as much as the destination."

"But if we're more efficient, we could spend our extra time back at the inn enjoying hot cocoa by the fire," Lila pressed. "Divide into teams of three or four, each take a section, and whoever finds the best tree calls the others over."

"Lila," Brady said, and she could tell by the way he said her name that it was a battle to not lose his patience with her, "not everything needs to be optimized. This is an honored tradition here, and it's one our guests look forward to."

Her face flushed with embarrassment as she caught the rest of the group watching the exchange with interest.

"Of course," Lila said quickly. "I didn't mean to try and take over. You all do this every year. I'm sure you know what you're doing."

Brady gave her a curt nod and then gestured for the group to follow him. So much for the momentary connection they'd had the night before.

Ali jumped in cheerfully as they walked toward the neighboring property. "I'm excited to see what kind of trees grow up here. The only place to get a tree in Miami is under a tent in the corner of a shopping center parking lot."

"The terrain is beautiful," added Tom. "Even if we don't find the perfect tree, the hike itself is worth it."

As they set off on the path through the woods, Lila found herself walking beside Brady, who carried the tools they'd need for cutting and securing the tree. The snow crunched beneath their boots, and she tried to find the words that could get them back to the truce they seemed to have found the night before.

"I'm sorry," she said quietly. "As you know, I have a tendency to try to solve problems that aren't actually problems."

"Maybe just remember that efficiency doesn't always have to be the goal. Let yourself live in the moment while you're here."

They walked in comfortable silence for a few minutes, following a worn path through the trees. Ahead of them, Miles pointed out different birds they spotted, while the sisters debated whether the snow was the right consistency to make snowballs.

"See what I mean?" Brady said. "If we'd split up, Miles wouldn't be teaching everyone about Steller's jays, and Kimberly and Kendall wouldn't be planning a snowball fight tournament for this afternoon."

Lila looked around at the group with new eyes. Sarah was walking with Carol; their heads bent together in quiet conversation. Tom was helping Sophie navigate a particularly icy patch of trail. Even though they'd only known each other for two days, they were starting to feel like their own little community.

"I think I'm beginning to get the hang of it," Lila said.

"Besides, if we found the tree too quickly, we'd miss out on the great tree debates," Brady added, his tone lighter. "Wait until you see how seriously people tend to take the selection process."

As if on cue, Kimberly called out from ahead. "Oh, what about this one?" She was standing beside a towering evergreen that had to be at least fourteen feet tall.

"Too big for the lobby," Carol called back. "Remember, it has to fit through the front door."

"And leave room for the star on top," added Miles.

"Plus, it's easier to decorate if we don't need a ladder," said Tom practically. "I don't want to have to drive anyone to the hospital because they leaned a little too far to the left to hang the perfect ornament."

Brady caught Lila's eye and raised his eyebrows as if to say, *See?*

They continued deeper into the woods, the group stopping every few minutes to consider and ultimately reject various trees. Too sparse, too lopsided, too small, wrong kind of pine. Lila found herself getting caught up in the process despite herself, offering opinions about the symmetry of the trees and whether the branches were strong enough to hold larger ornaments.

After about thirty minutes of hiking and tree evaluation, they reached a small clearing where several promising candidates stood nearby.

"This is where we usually take a break," Brady told the group, pulling a thermos from his backpack. "Anyone ready for hot apple cider?"

As the group gathered, passing around the thermos and paper cups, Sarah settled onto a fallen log with a wistful expression.

"Are you okay?" Lila asked as she sat beside her.

Sarah nodded. "This just brings back memories," she said, scanning the trees around them.

"You've been here for past Christmases, right?" Ali asked.

Sarah nodded, her fingers absently tracing patterns in the snow beside her. "Yes, for many years now, but I was just thinking about my first time here, actually. I came with my husband during Christmas of 1990. We rented a little cabin in town for the week and decided we needed a tree to make it feel like home."

"How romantic," sighed Kimberly. "Did you pick a good one?"

"We found a beautiful little tree, about six feet tall with perfect symmetry." Sarah's voice grew soft with memory. "David was so particular about it. He said it had to be just right because we were going to make it a tradition, coming to Pine Ridge every Christmas and picking our tree out here together."

No one said anything, waiting for her to continue. "We only had that one Christmas together though. David got sick and passed away a few months later."

The group fell quiet, the only sounds the whisper of wind through the pine branches and the distant call of a bird. Lila felt her chest tighten with recognition of that particular kind of grief.

"I'm so sorry," Ali said softly, and the others murmured their agreement.

"Thank you," Sarah said. "It was a long time ago, but that Christmas here was so magical that I started coming back."

"And we love having you," Carol said, sitting beside Sarah and putting an arm around her.

"Well," said Tom, clearing his throat gently. "Should we find ourselves a tree worthy of another special Pine Ridge Christmas?"

The group rose from their impromptu rest, but Lila noticed how Sarah's eyes lingered on the trees around them, as if she was seeing more than just the present moment.

They resumed their search with renewed purpose, and it was Brady who spotted the winner. "What about this one?" he called from the edge of the clearing.

The tree he'd found was perhaps eight feet tall with full, evenly spaced branches that would hold ornaments beautifully. It wasn't the biggest or most dramatic tree they'd seen, but it had a perfect, classic Christmas tree shape.

"Oh, it's lovely," breathed Carol.

"The branches are strong enough for heavy ornaments," observed Tom.

"And it's exactly the right height for the lobby," added Miles.

Brady looked at Lila expectantly. "What do you think? Does this one pass the test?"

Lila walked around the tree, studying it from all angles. It was beautiful, but more than that, it felt right. Standing there in the clearing with a few snowflakes beginning to fall softly around them and the group gathered in anticipation, she finally understood what Brady had been trying to tell her. It was about the journey, not the destination, as the old saying went.

"I think it's perfect," she said, and meant it.

"Excellent," said Brady, pulling the saw from his pack.

Lila found herself watching the strong line of Brady's jaw as he concentrated on each motion. When a piece of dark hair slipped from beneath his hat to brush his forehead, she had the unexpected urge to reach out and push it back. She wasn't interested in any kind of holiday fling, but it didn't hurt to just look.

When the tree finally fell with a soft whoosh into the snow, the group cheered.

"Now comes the fun part," Brady said, producing a length of rope. "Getting it back to the inn."

They worked as a team to secure the tree for transport, with different people taking turns carrying the trunk end while others guided the branches. Lila found herself walking beside Brady again, both of them holding the rope that kept the tree stable.

"This was great," she said as they made their way back through the woods. "You were right about the search being half the fun."

"You don't have to sound so surprised that my way turned out to be the best way." He gave her a teasing smile. "You might give hotels advice for a living, but I run one for a living."

She gave him a sheepish smile. "Touché."

As they emerged from the woods with their prize, Lila felt something she hadn't experienced in months: a sense of belonging somewhere. The tree selection had been about more than finding decoration for the inn's lobby. It had been about connecting with others and creating a small moment of magic together.

Back at the inn, they maneuvered the tree through the front door and into the lobby, where it would wait until the evening's decorating party. The group dispersed to warm up and change clothes, their cheeks red from the cold and their spirits high from the morning's success.

Lila was heading upstairs when Carol called her name from the front desk.

"You have a message, dear," Carol said as she hung up the phone. "Cynthia from the yarn shop called about twenty minutes ago. She asked if you could stop by this afternoon when you have a chance."

Lila's heart began to race. After the peaceful morning in the woods, she'd almost forgotten about the real reason she'd come to Pine Ridge. But now, Cynthia's message had all her anxiety rushing back.

She thought she'd wanted Cynthia to find something, but now she wasn't so sure. Her birth mother had never unsealed the records. So why was Lila trying to find someone who clearly didn't want to be found? Suddenly, she didn't feel ready for what might come next.

Seven

L ila stood at her bedroom window, watching snowflakes drift past the glass as she wrestled with her decision. Cynthia's simple request for Lila to come by the store felt loaded with possibility. After the morning tree hunt, when she'd felt genuinely happy for the first time in months, the weight of her real purpose in Pine Ridge pressed on her chest like a stone.

What if the yarn shop owner had found nothing? What if she'd found something Lila wasn't ready to hear?

Finally, she grabbed her coat. Lila had come to Pine Ridge for answers, and hiding in her room wouldn't get her any closer to them.

The walk to Emily's Yarn & Quilts took only a few minutes, and part of her wished it had taken longer so she had more time to weigh the possibilities. Through the shop's front window, she could see Cynthia arranging a display of yarn. When the bell chimed above the door, Cynthia looked up with a warm smile.

"Lila! I'm so glad you came by." Cynthia set down the skein of red wool she'd been holding and moved toward the counter. "I found something in my mother's journals."

Lila's heart began to race. "You did?"

"It wasn't much, but it was something." Cynthia pulled a worn leather journal from beneath the counter, its pages yellowed with age. "My mother was very methodical about recording her commissioned pieces."

She opened the journal to a page marked with a ribbon bookmark, her finger tracing down entries written in faded blue ink. "Here it is. 'December 15th, 1991. Baby quilt, red, green, and white squares with patterned accents. Rush order, completed December 24th. Delivered to Pine Ridge Inn.'"

The words hit Lila like a physical blow. "Pine Ridge Inn? You mean where I'm staying?"

"That's what it says." Cynthia's expression was gentle but curious. "I have to admit, I was surprised. Most of my mother's baby quilts were picked up by the customers themselves or occasionally delivered to homes. But this one went to the inn."

Lila stared at the journal entry, her mind racing. Did that mean her birth mother didn't live in Pine Ridge and was only passing through when she'd gone into labor?

"There's no name or other information?" she asked.

"I'm afraid not. My mother didn't include those details on this one, just what was made and where it went." Cynthia studied Lila's face with concern. "Are you all right, dear? You look a bit pale."

"I'm fine," Lila said quickly, though she felt anything but fine. "Thank you so much for looking into this. It's more than I had before."

"I wish I could tell you more. I know how important this must be to you." Cynthia closed the journal carefully. "I hope you're able to find what you're looking for."

As she walked back toward the inn, Lila's mind churned with new possibilities. The quilt had been delivered to Pine Ridge Inn in December 1991. She knew from one of their dinner conversations that Tom and Carol started dating several years after Carol began working at the inn as a front desk clerk back when Tom's parents ran things. Maybe they would remember a guest who was pregnant that year and went into labor on Christmas Day? Surely that would be hard to forget.

Lila suddenly stopped walking. She remembered Tom saying he fell in love with Carol the first time he saw her but that she'd been with the local "bad boy" when she first came to work at the inn. And Carol had mentioned at one point how much she'd always wanted children but that it hadn't been in the cards.

Could it have been Carol who ordered the quilt for a baby she was planning to give up for adoption? Had she gotten pregnant by a boyfriend who hadn't stuck around and decided to give the baby up before eventually settling down with Tom?

The swirling thoughts made Lila's chest tight with a mixture of hope and terror. It was a long shot, but she couldn't help picturing it. Carol seemed so wonderful. After all, look what she'd done for Brady when he'd lost his mother.

Lost in thought, Lila climbed the stairs to the inn's front door. Through the windows, she could see the group gathered around a table, their heads bent over what ap-

peared to be craft supplies. She'd missed the start of ornament making while she was at the yarn shop.

The lobby was quiet when she entered, but voices and
laughter drifted from the dining room. She stood in the
doorway for a moment, watching the scene unfold. Brady
was helping Sophie thread a needle while Tom demonstrated how to make a paper snowflake. The sisters were
deep in debate over whether silver or gold ribbon looked
better on their pinecone ornaments. Sarah sat beside Carol, carefully stitching what looked like a tiny felt star.

Lila found herself studying Carol with new intensity.
Carol's reddish-blonde hair caught the light as she leaned
over her work, her expression focused but peaceful. Lila's
hair was blonde, but it had red undertones her stylist was
always having to combat so her blonde highlights didn't
turn brassy.

Carol had kind eyes with laugh lines that made her look
wise—and dare Lila say, maternal. Could this warm, caring woman really be the one who'd carried Lila for nine
months and then made the impossible choice to let her go?

"Lila!" Kimberly called out, looking up from a half-fin-
ished ornament that appeared to involve entirely too much
glitter. "Perfect timing. We saved you a spot."

"And some supplies," added Kendall, gesturing to an
empty chair beside Sarah. "Though I'd avoid the glitter if
you don't want to sparkle for the next six months. I swear,
it sticks to everything." Indeed, Kendall's cheek sparkled
from a swipe of stray glitter.

"Don't listen to her," Kimberly protested. "Glitter
makes everything better."

"You say that now," Brady said with amusement, "but
wait until you find it in your coffee tomorrow morning."

Despite her racing thoughts, Lila found herself smiling as she took the empty seat. Sarah handed her a basket filled with felt scraps, ribbons, and various craft supplies.

"I was just starting a little angel," Sarah said, showing Lila her work in progress. "Though I'm not sure my sewing skills are up to the task."

"It's beautiful," Lila said, admiring the delicate stitching. "I'm not sure I have any artistic ability at all."

"Nonsense," Carol said from across the table, looking up from her own project. "Everyone has creativity in them. Sometimes it just takes the right project to bring it out."

Lila selected a piece of deep green felt and began cutting out a simple tree shape, but her attention kept drifting to Carol. Every gesture, every expression, every word felt loaded with new meaning. When Carol laughed at one of Tom's jokes, Lila found herself analyzing the sound, looking for some echo of familiarity. When Carol offered to help Ali with a complicated folding technique, Lila watched her hands, searching for some genetic similarity. Were her fingers long like Lila's? Lila's mother always said she should have taken up playing the piano because of her long, graceful fingers.

"That's coming along nicely," Carol said, moving around the table to check on everyone's progress. When she reached Lila, she paused, her eyes warm with approval. Lila was just beginning to add a yellow star she'd cut out. "I love the simplicity of it. Sometimes the most beautiful ornaments are the ones that don't try too hard."

The compliment made Lila's chest flutter with an emotion she couldn't quite name. "Thank you. I'm not much of a crafter, but there's something soothing about it."

"My mother always said that working with your hands quiets the mind," Carol said, settling back into her chair. "She taught me to sew when I was young, and I've always found it meditative."

"Did you make quilts too?" Lila asked,

"No, but my mother did." Carol's expression grew fond. "She loved making quilts for wedding gifts to celebrate the newlyweds. It's probably part of the reason I gravitated to Emily and Cynthia when I moved here. I used to just go stand in their shop and study the quilts. Emily tried to teach me how to make a baby quilt one time, but I couldn't quite get the hang of it. She always said those baby quilts were her favorite because they carried so much hope."

Lila's hand stilled on her ornament. "Baby quilts?"

"Mm-hmm." She looked at Brady. "You have one your mother commissioned from Emily, right?"

Brady nodded. "Yeah, it's somewhere in all my stuff. I think maybe it would cover the bottom half of my legs these days. All the kids I knew in town had one though. It's a rite of passage around here, I guess."

"That sounds like a lovely legacy," Lila managed.

"I heard her say one time that each stitch held a prayer for the baby who would use it," Carol said. "I always thought that was a really beautiful sentiment."

A soft clatter interrupted the moment as Sarah's scissors slipped from her fingers and hit the table. "Oh, sorry," she murmured, quickly retrieving them. "How clumsy of me."

Carol glanced at Sarah for a moment, then cleared her throat softly. "Well, enough of my rambling about old times. Let's see what everyone else is making!"

The conversation moved on to other topics, but Lila barely heard it. She couldn't stop imagining a younger Carol, abandoned by her boyfriend and feeling too young to care for a child on her own. Lila had always imagined—or maybe just hoped—that her mother had given her up in some selfless act of care for her. If she simply hadn't wanted her, why would she have gone to the trouble of sending along the quilt and other items with her? It sounded exactly like something Carol would do.

The afternoon passed in a blur of cutting and stitching and half-heard conversation. Lila managed to complete her simple tree ornament and even started a second one, but her attention remained fixed on Carol. Every word, every gesture, every interaction felt like a clue she could decode if she only tried hard enough.

When dinner time arrived, the group reluctantly packed away their craft supplies to make room for the evening meal. Lila barely touched her food, too distracted by the possibility that she might be sitting across the table from her birth mother. Carol seemed to sense her distraction, offering gentle smiles and checking if she needed anything, which only made the sense that they were connected in some way feel even stronger.

After dinner, the group gathered in the lobby to decorate the tree they'd cut that morning. Brady had set it up in the corner by the fireplace, and it stood tall and proud, waiting for their handmade ornaments. The scene was exactly what someone might picture when they thought of a perfect Christmas evening with friends gathered around a beautiful tree, firelight dancing on the walls, the scent of pine filling the air.

Tom began stringing lights while the rest of them organized ornaments. There were the ones they'd made that afternoon, plus boxes of decorations that had clearly accumulated over many years. Some looked handmade by previous guests, others appeared to be family heirlooms, and still others seemed to have stories attached that only Carol and Tom knew.

"Oh, here's one of my favorites," Carol said, lifting a delicate glass angel from the tissue paper. "This was made by a guest about fifteen years ago who'd come with her parents for many years. She came the first Christmas after her mother passed and said she could feel her here and wanted to leave this angel behind to watch over the inn."

Lila's chest squeezed as she thought of last Christmas with her own mother. She wished she'd known it would be their last. She would have treasured every moment a little more. Remembered more of the stories her mother had told about their ornaments as they hung them. Taken more pictures. Stayed up later watching old Christmas movies. But she'd taken it for granted and assumed they'd have another holiday just like it this year. Tears burned her eyes, but she blinked them away.

Sarah seemed to notice Lila's reaction to the ornament and leaned over to whisper, "You okay?"

"Mmm hmm," Lila said, unable to say more at the risk of bursting into tears. So far, Brady was the only one she'd told about her mother, and she hadn't really planned to broadcast it to the rest. If they all pitied or fussed over her, it would only make it worse.

Lila managed to distract herself with a debate Ali and Kendall were having over whether the ornament they were holding made by a previous guest was meant to be a wolf or a dog. Carol and Tom shared stories about many of the decorations from previous years, including the beloved guests who'd made them. Kendall was hoping they'd come across something they remembered from their childhood Christmases at the inn, but Kimberly reminded her they'd taken those home to put on their own tree.

Lila was hanging her creations from the day when Kimberly pulled a small ornament from the bottom of one of the boxes. It was tiny, clearly delicate, and when she held it up to the light, Lila could see it was a silver rattle with "Baby's First Christmas" engraved on it.

Carol looked up from where she was removing another item from the box, her expression shifting to something deeply sad. Tom noticed her stillness and moved to her side, his hand gently touching her shoulder.

"I'm sorry," Kimberly said, handing the rattle to Carol. "Is this one personal?"

"In a way," Carol said, her voice soft. "Sometimes the most important people in our lives are the ones we carry in our hearts rather than hold in our arms."

Lila was frozen in place, watching as Carol hung the ornament, Tom staying close at her side with his hand on the small of her back in a way that was both protective and comforting.

Carol's cryptic answer only fueled Lila's speculation. She wanted to ask more, to push for details, but something in Carol's expression warned her that this was sacred ground, not to be trespassed upon lightly.

The rest of the ornament hanging continued with slightly subdued energy, the group seeming to sense that Carol and Tom had shared something private and meaningful. When they finally stepped back to admire their work, the tree stood tall and proud in the corner, each ornament catching and reflecting the firelight.

"It's perfect," breathed Ali. "I've never seen a more beautiful Christmas tree."

"We make a pretty good team," agreed Miles, his arm around Sophie's shoulders.

Brady surveyed their work with satisfaction. "I think this might be our best one yet. What do you think, Carol?"

Carol wiped her eyes once more, then smiled with genuine warmth. "I think it's perfect. Thank you all for making this so special."

As the evening wound down and people began drifting toward their rooms, Lila lingered by the tree. The baby ornament caught the light, its silver surface gleaming among the handmade decorations they'd added that day. She found herself staring at it, wondering about its story and about Carol's reaction.

"Thinking about how we could have decorated it more efficiently?" Brady teased as he appeared beside her.

"Very funny," she deadpanned. "No, just taking it all in. This trip hasn't been exactly what I expected."

"What did you expect?"

"Honestly? I thought I'd spend the week hiding in my room, avoiding Christmas altogether." She laughed softly. "Instead, I'm making ornaments and picking trees and feeling like . . ."

"Like what?"

"Like maybe I was meant to be here this Christmas." She paused, considering whether to share the next part. "Like maybe the first Christmas without my mother doesn't have to be completely miserable."

Brady's expression softened. "If it makes you feel any better, I lost both of my parents at the same time, and I survived that first Christmas. In fact, I spent it right here, so I'd say you're on the right track." He said it in a light tone, suggesting maybe he was the type that handled sadness with jokes and self-deprecating humor.

She knew about his parents already thanks to Sarah, but she was surprised he'd said it. Maybe, like her, it was nice to find someone else who understood.

"You lost your parents at the same time? I'm sorry."

He turned from the tree and walked toward the fire, so she followed.

"Both my parents were killed in a car accident just before my junior year of high school." He said it matter-of-factly, but Lila could hear the old pain underneath the composed exterior.

"That must have been devastating." It had been bad enough when Lila had lost her parents so close together. She couldn't imagine losing them at the exact same time.

"It was. One day I had a normal family and plans for college, and the next day it was all gone." Brady was quiet for a long moment as he poked at the logs on the fire. "Tom and Carol were my parents' best friends. When they found out I didn't want to move to Florida to live with my uncle when I was so close to graduation, they didn't hesitate to take me in."

"That's incredible. What amazing people." Lila wasn't at all surprised to learn they'd done something so selfless. They certainly seemed like the type of people who always took care of others.

Brady nodded. "The cabin I'm in used to just be storage, but they let me move in after my parents passed so I'd feel like I had my own space."

"Most people wouldn't trust a teenager on their own like that. I guess that means you didn't have a curfew?" she joked. "My mom still waited up for me to come in when I was home visiting, even into my thirties."

"No." He smiled as he sat on the hearth. "No curfew. Between school and work, I was too busy to get into much trouble anyway." He studied her face.

"Sounds like you had to grow up fast."

Brady shrugged. "Maybe, but it's what I needed at the time. Tom taught me everything about running this place, and Carol made sure I didn't lose myself in my grief. She'd find projects for me when I was struggling or just sit with me when she could sense I didn't want to be alone."

Lila felt her chest tighten with recognition. "You're lucky to have found people who cared that much."

Brady went on to describe all the things the Brennans had done to keep his family alive for him. Carol cooked his favorite—pot roast—for his birthday every year, just like his mother had. Tom learned how to fly fish because it had been Brady's pastime with his father.

"Can I make an observation?"

"I don't recall you having any problem speaking your mind before, so why stop now?" he teased her, his lips curling into a smile at the corners.

She huffed out a small laugh at his ribbing before her tone turned serious. "It sounds like the Brennans stepped in where your parents left off, but in a way that was comforting without being overbearing. But did you ever feel like you were replacing your real family?" She knew the question was more about the mixed feelings she had over her current endeavor to find her birth mother than it was about him, but she was genuinely curious how he'd handled it all.

"No." His answer was immediate and firm. "My parents will always be my parents. But I learned that family isn't just about blood—it's about the people who choose to walk alongside you in life. Tom and Carol didn't try to replace my parents. They just made room for me in their family."

Is that how she would be received by her birth mother? With open arms? If it was Carol, it seemed like a fair bet. Maybe that's why she was beginning to hope it was true.

But what if it wasn't Carol? Would her birth mother be married? Would she have other children now? And how would they react to Lila's appearance in their lives?

Even worse, what if there was no family? No mother to find. What if she was gone now and Lila had waited too long?

Her mind swirling and eyes stinging with tears, Lila suddenly couldn't sit still any longer. "I should probably get some sleep," she said as she stood.

"Good night, Lila," Brady said, his voice gentle and low. "For what it's worth, I think you came to the right place this year."

She could only nod in reply as she turned so he wouldn't see the tears threatening to spill over. As she climbed the stairs to her room, her mind churned with all the unanswered questions. The biggest one of all: Was she really ready to discover all the truths?

Back in her room, Lila sat on the edge of the bed and pulled out her phone, scrolling to Jenna's number. Her finger hovered over her friend's name. Jenna would be busy with family in town. She pressed call before she could second-guess herself anymore. She had to talk to someone.

"Please tell me you're not hiding in your room eating room service," Jenna teased as she answered.

"I'm not hiding in my room eating room service," Lila said, settling back against her pillows. Just hearing Jenna's voice calmed her nerves. "Though I am kind of hungry, because I was too distracted at dinner to eat."

"Distracted by what? And please tell me it involves some handsome lumberjack you met in the woods."

"That sounds more like the beginning of a slasher film than a love story," Lila joked as her mood lightened. "I'm not out here wandering the woods alone hoping to run into some random man."

"Shame," Jenna said. "That whole rugged, outdoorsman thing is really hot. Trust me." Jenna's husband was a firefighter who spent his weekends hiking, kayaking, or otherwise communing with nature. And she was right; he was hot. You know, as much as your best friend's husband could be.

"Well . . ." Lila teased as she pictured Brady's muscles stretching the fabric of his flannel shirt while he was chopping down the Christmas tree, "there is actually a rugged, outdoorsy kind of guy right here at the inn." At the moment, she'd rather talk about Brady than why she'd really called.

"Spill," Jenna demanded. "I want to hear all about him."

Lila told her about how she'd clashed with Brady at first as she made suggestions about the inn but how he'd opened up that evening about his parents.

"Sounds like you two have a lot in common, from your work to your family situation."

"He's surprisingly easy to talk to," she admitted. "At least he is now that he's decided I'm not trying to ruin his inn."

"Uh huh. And I bet he looks pretty good in those flannel shirts and hiking boots too, huh?"

Lila felt heat rise to her cheeks, glad Jenna couldn't see her blushing through the phone. "I mean, objectively, he's not unattractive . . ." Lila hedged.

"Does he have a girlfriend?"

"Jenna! I'm here to look for clues about my birth mother, not go on dates with the manager of the inn." Although now that she thought about it, he hadn't mentioned anyone, and surely he would have some holiday obligations with her if he had one.

"Who says you can't do both? Come on, when's the last time you had a crush on a guy? This is good for you!"

"I don't have a crush. I'm just . . . intrigued by him." Lila took a deep breath. "But that's not why I called. I need a pep talk."

Jenna's voice shifted, sensing the seriousness in Lila's tone. "Okay, spill. What's going on?"

She told Jenna about Cynthia's discovery that the quilt had been delivered to Pine Ridge Inn and about her growing suspicion that Carol might be her birth mother. Jenna listened without interrupting, making occasional sounds of encouragement.

"So, what are you going to do?" Jenna asked when Lila finished.

"I don't know. I can't just walk up to her and ask if she gave birth to a baby on Christmas Day thirty-four years ago, can I?"

"Probably not the best opening line," Jenna agreed. "But Lila, what if she is? What if you found her?"

"That's what terrifies me. What if I did, and what if she doesn't want anything to do with me? What if seeing me just brings up painful memories she'd rather forget?"

"Or what if she's been hoping for this moment for thirty-four years?"

Lila pressed her free hand to her forehead. "I don't know how to handle this, Jen. I came here thinking I'd find some clues, then I'd go back and do an internet search and study the person online before I contacted them. I don't think I gave enough thought to her actually being here and what it would be like to actually approach someone and ask if she's my birth mother."

Jenna was quiet for a moment, considering. "First of all, you don't even know if Carol is your birth mother. Second, even if she is, that doesn't mean anything terrible will happen. Maybe she'll be thrilled to see you. Don't get ahead of yourself, okay? Just take things one step at a time."

"You're right," Lila said, sighing. "I'm probably over-thinking this whole thing."

"Overthinking is your specialty," Jenna teased gently. "Why don't you just get to know her better and maybe start dropping some hints and see if she picks up on them?"

It wasn't a bad idea. She didn't have to let on that she had any ideas about Carol being her mother. She could just subtly start sharing more about why she was in town and see if Carol picked up on it.

"Yeah, I could do that. Thanks, Jen. I just needed to talk it out with someone."

"I'm proud of you for taking this step, Lila. For going there in the first place. Whatever happens, I'm here for you."

"Thanks. I think I needed to hear that."

They talked for a few more minutes about lighter things—Jenna's mother-in-law nagging her, Lila's description of the ornament-making afternoon, the ridiculous amount of glitter Kimberly had managed to get on everything within a three-foot radius.

"I should let you go," Jenna said finally. "The monster-in-law is probably reorganizing my pantry she thinks I don't keep organized enough. But remember, one step at a time, okay? And keep me posted on the Brady situation too. I expect a full report next time we talk!"

Lila laughed. "Aye, aye, Captain."

"And remember, just try being in the moment."

After she hung up, Lila felt marginally better about the situation. Jenna was right. She was getting ahead of herself. She didn't even know for certain that Carol was her birth mother. All she had were coincidences and speculation.

Tomorrow, she would have to decide how to reveal to Carol why she'd really come to Pine Ridge. Tonight, she just had to figure out how to sleep while her world potentially shifted around her.

Outside her window, snow continued to fall on the quiet town. Somewhere in Pine Ridge was the answer to the question that had brought her here.

Eight

The morning of the Pine Ridge Christmas Festival dawned crisp and clear, with fresh snow sparkling on the rooftops like crystallized sugar atop gingerbread houses. Lila stood at her window, watching the town come alive as vendors set up booths along Main Street and others strung additional lights between the old-fashioned street-lamps.

She'd barely slept, her mind churning with questions about Carol and the baby ornament and the growing certainty that she was closer to answers than she'd ever been. Every time she'd drifted off, she'd jolted awake with new scenarios playing in her mind—conversations with Carol that revealed the truth, or worse, conversations that shattered her hopes entirely.

A soft knock interrupted her thoughts. Lila opened the door to find Sarah holding two steaming mugs. She was dressed in a cream-colored sweater and burgundy scarf that brought out the warmth in her brown eyes.

"I missed you for our morning coffee today. I thought you might need this before we head out to the festival," Sarah said, holding out a cup to Lila.

Lila had purposely stayed in her room to try and calm her nerves, but now she regretted skipping what had become her morning ritual at the inn. It warmed her heart to think Sarah had wanted her there.

"You're an angel," Lila said, accepting the coffee gratefully and motioning for Sarah to come in. "I was just watching everyone get set up. It looks like the whole town is involved."

"Pretty much," Sarah agreed, settling into the wingback chair by the window. "That's one of the things I love about Pine Ridge. When they do something, they do it together."

Lila sat on the edge of the bed, cradling her mug and studying Sarah's face. There was something about her presence that made Lila feel calmer, more centered. "How long have you been coming here for Christmas?"

"Oh, quite a few years now. After David passed, I tried spending holidays with various family members, but it never felt right. Too much forced cheer, too many people trying to fix my sadness." Sarah's expression grew distant. "But here, people let you be where you are. They don't try to rush you through those complicated feelings about the holiday or pretend it doesn't exist."

"It's exactly what I needed this year," Lila admitted. "I lost my mother back in the spring, and the thought of Christmas without her . . ."

Sarah's eyes filled with understanding. "Oh honey, I'm so sorry. The first Christmas after losing someone you love is brutal."

"How did you get through it?"

"The only way you can, one moment at a time. And by letting people like Carol and Tom take care of me, even when I wanted to push everyone away." Sarah reached over and squeezed Lila's hand. "There's something about this place that helps you remember that you're not alone, even when you feel like you are."

The gesture was so maternal, so naturally comforting, that Lila felt tears prick her eyes. "Thank you. For understanding, I mean. And for the coffee and the company."

"Of course," Sarah said warmly. "We have to look out for each other."

Downstairs a short while later, the lobby buzzed with excitement as the group prepared for their day at the festival. Carol moved among them with her usual energy, checking that everyone had warm enough clothes and coordinating meeting times.

"The craft booths open at nine," Carol said, "but I recommend getting there early for the best selection."

"I hope we find some good gifts for Mom and Dad," Kendall said to Kimberly. "I didn't have any time to shop before we left town."

"Me either," Kimberly said. "I'm sure there will be plenty to choose from."

"Absolutely," Carol assured them. "There are beautiful wood carvings, paintings, jewelry, pottery, you name it. Pine Ridge has quite an artistic community." Carol's eyes lit up with pride for her town. "And the bakery serves hot chocolate and cinnamon rolls in their booth, which I highly recommend."

Brady appeared from the kitchen, carrying a thermos. "You had me at cinnamon rolls," he said, grinning.

"Maybe we should do a quick turn around the festival before we leave," Ali said to Mike, who had just descended the stairs with their ski gear. They were spending the day skiing in nearby Breckenridge.

"Not a chance." Mike shook his head, smiling. "You'll see something in a booth and get distracted and we'll never make it to the slopes."

Ali laughed. "You're probably right."

"I made you two a little breakfast picnic to go," Carol said, picking up a basket from the front desk filled with muffins, apples, and bananas.

"You're the best." Ali gave Carol a big hug as she accepted the basket.

"What I wouldn't give to go skiing again," Sophie said wistfully. "Get out there and 'shred some powder,' as you kids say, while you're still young enough to do it."

"I could still ski," Miles said. "I saw a guy in the paper the other day who was still skiing at eighty."

"Not with your two titanium knees and that hip replacement," Sophie said, shaking her head.

"That's precisely why I could do it," he argued. "Nothing left to break."

"I'm sure you could find something." She laughed, looping her arm in his. "Come with me, and I'll buy you one of those cinnamon rolls."

Brady came to stand beside Lila as Sophie and Miles continued to tease each other. "Everything okay? You're quiet this morning."

"Just excited about the festival," she said. Anxious was more like it. She planned to spend as much time as possible today with Carol to see what she could uncover.

He furrowed his brows, clearly not buying her explanation. She was relieved when he didn't push it any further, and then Tom pulled him away to help load some things they were taking down to the festival.

Twenty minutes later, Lila made her way with the rest of the group down Main Street toward the heart of the festival. The transformation was remarkable—as if they'd gone to sleep last night in quiet Pine Ridge and awoke this morning at the North Pole. Booths lined both sides of the street, their red and green banners fluttering in the light breeze. The scent of cinnamon and hot apple cider drifted from food vendors, mixing with the crisp mountain air and the ever-present smell of pine.

"It's magical," Lila breathed, taking in the scene. Families with small children moved between booths, couples walked hand in hand, and elderly residents sat on benches watching the activity with obvious contentment as they warmed their hands on paper cups filled with steaming refreshments.

"Wait until you see it tonight," Sarah said as she came up beside Lila. "They light up the whole street for the tree ceremony, and it looks like something from a storybook."

They walked slowly, stopping to admire displays of handcrafted goods. At a woodworking booth, an elderly man demonstrated carving techniques while his wife arranged ornate jewelry boxes and cutting boards. A few booths down, a woman in her thirties sold homemade soaps and candles with seasonal scents like balsam and gingerbread.

"Sarah! Lila!" Carol's voice called from across the street. She was standing with Tom beside a booth displaying quilts and other textile crafts—Cynthia's booth, Lila realized with a start.

They made their way over, weaving through clusters of festivalgoers. Cynthia looked up from arranging a display of baby quilts and smiled warmly when she saw Lila.

"How lovely to see you again," Cynthia said. "What do you think of our little festival?"

"It's wonderful," Lila replied, acutely aware of Carol and Sarah listening to their exchange and hoping Cynthia wouldn't mention the quilt. "The whole town really comes together for this."

"It's been a tradition for over fifty years," Carol said proudly. "Tom's grandfather actually started it as a way to bring the community together during the holidays. Back then it was much smaller, just a few families selling crafts and sharing food."

"How long have you lived here, Carol?" Lila asked, seizing the opportunity. "You seem to know so much about the town's history."

"Oh, most of my adult life. I came here in my early twenties and never left." Carol's expression grew fond as she looked around at the bustling street. "This place has a way of getting into your heart."

"Did you grow up in Colorado?"

"Born and raised in Denver, but I needed a change of scenery after high school, so I came out to work at the ski resort over in Breckenridge. Small-town life suited me much better than the city." Carol fingered a quilt on Cynthia's display, her touch gentle. "Though I'll admit, my first few years here were a bit challenging. I was young and made some poor choices in the romance department."

Cynthia and Carol exchanged a glance Lila couldn't read, and it occurred to Lila that Cynthia would have known if Carol had given up a child. Had she purposely not given Lila more details? Only told Lila about the delivery to the inn so Lila would question Carol? Had Cynthia warned Carol? Maybe Carol was assessing Lila the same way Lila was assessing her. Would she measure up enough for Carol to tell her the truth?

Lila was spiraling. She fingered her mother's sapphire ring she wore on her right hand, trying to conjure the quiet sense of calm her mother had always embodied.

She needed to keep this conversation going. It was the only way she was going to get to the truth.

"Poor choices how?" Lila asked, trying to keep her tone casual.

"Oh, you know how it is when you're young. You fall for the wrong type of guy—the one your parents warn you about." Carol's laugh was rueful. "He was charming and exciting, but not exactly the settling-down type. I learned that lesson the hard way."

Lila's heart began to race. This sounded exactly like the backstory she'd imagined for her birth mother. "That must have been difficult."

"It was, at the time. But it led me to Tom eventually, so I can't regret it completely." Carol's expression softened as she looked toward her husband, who was examining a hand-carved nativity set at the next booth. "Sometimes the hardest experiences teach us what we really want."

Lila wracked her brain for a tactful way to ask Carol something that might lead to the story behind the silver baby rattle hanging on the tree back at the inn. Then she spotted a baby quilt in Cynthia's display, not unlike hers.

"Isn't this just precious," Lila said, leaning over to observe it more closely. She glanced toward Cynthia, worried about the connection to her own quilt, but thankfully Cynthia was busy attending to another customer who'd walked up to the side of the booth.

"How sweet," Sophie said, coming up to join them. "I should buy one for my son and daughter-in-law. They're expecting their first."

"Congratulations," Carol said, but her smile didn't quite reach her eyes. "Your first grandchild, what a blessing."

"It is," Sophie said. "She's been trying for a couple of years and was just getting ready to try IVF when it happened the old-fashioned way. Poor thing had a miscarriage early on, so we all held our breaths the first few months of this one."

Carol's eyes were welling with tears as she fingered the edge of the baby quilt. "Tom and I tried for years after we got married, but it just wasn't meant to be. Sometimes I think about the children we might have had, wonder what they would have been like."

Lila's heart sped up. Had Carol gotten pregnant with the "bad boy" boyfriend and given the baby—her—up for adoption and then regretted it when she couldn't have children with Tom? She wracked her brain for a way to ask that wasn't obvious, but she came up short.

"You would have been a wonderful mother, sweetheart," Sophie said, placing a hand on Carol's arm. "That must have been heartbreaking."

"It was. Still is, sometimes. But you learn to find family in other ways." Carol's smile returned, but a single tear streaked down her cheek. "Tom and I have been blessed with so many wonderful people in our lives though—Brady, our guests who return year after year, friends like Sarah here."

Sarah had a faraway look in her eyes, and Lila wondered if she was regretting that she never had children. It didn't sound like she'd had much interest in remarrying after her husband passed, even though she'd still been young.

She recovered, and Sarah reached out to squeeze Carol's hand. "And we've been blessed to have you both."

"Should we look at some of these other booths?" Carol asked, forcing a smile. "I want to show you the pottery display. Martha's work is absolutely stunning, and she always has some items that make great gifts."

The conversation had started even better than Lila could have scripted it, but she hadn't been able to steer it where she wanted it to go. Now, Lila couldn't push further without seeming rude or unfeeling. She'd have to find another way later.

They spent the next hour browsing various displays. Carol was in her element, greeting vendors and festival-goers by name, sharing stories about different artisans and their work. She was clearly beloved by the community, stopping every few minutes to chat with friends or admire someone's children.

"Carol's really something special, isn't she?" Sarah said quietly as they watched Carol kneel to talk to a little girl who was showing off her face painting.

"She really is," Lila agreed. "I can see why you keep coming back here. She and Tom make everyone feel like family."

"They do." Sarah's voice was soft with affection. "Carol especially has this gift for seeing what people need and providing it, even when they don't ask."

They continued walking, and Lila found herself studying every interaction Carol had, looking for clues about her past. All she saw, however, was a woman beloved by her community who remembered even the smallest details of each of their lives, asking about their pets, children, and grandchildren all by name. Sophie was right that Carol would have been a wonderful mom. But Lila had a wonderful mom, and maybe the most motherly thing of all had been Carol knowing she couldn't be that mom when the time had come, even if she had become that person later.

By midday, they'd made their way through most of the booths and were settling at a picnic table with hot cider and festival food. The rest of the group had caught up with them, and the table was full of chatter about their various purchases and discoveries.

"The woodworking booth had some beautiful pieces," Sophie was saying. "I bought a jewelry box for my daughter."

"And did you see the handmade ornaments at the far end?" Kimberly added. "I may have gone a little overboard, but they were all so unique."

Brady appeared with a tray piled high with food, having finished his morning volunteer duties. "How's everyone enjoying the festival?"

"It's wonderful," Kendall said. "I can't believe how much talent there is in such a small town."

"Wait until tonight," Brady said, settling beside Lila on the bench in the only open seat. "The tree lighting ceremony is really something to see."

"Will the whole town be there?" Lila asked.

"Pretty much. It's the highlight of the holiday season here."

Brady's shoulder brushed hers as he reached for his drink, and she felt a flutter of awareness. She silently cursed Jenna for planting the hot lumberjack seed in her head.

"Carol usually says a few words before they light the tree, since she's been so involved in organizing the festival over the years," Brady continued.

Sarah nodded. "Carol has such a gift for bringing people together. I think she understands better than most how precious these connections are."

"What do you mean?" Lila asked.

Sarah seemed to choose her words carefully. "I just think when you've experienced loss or difficulty, you develop a deeper appreciation for the people who show up for you. Carol's been through her share of challenges, and it's made her incredibly generous with others."

Before Lila could ask what kind of challenges Sarah meant, Tom appeared at their table.

"Carol sent me to round everyone up," he said with a grin. "The caroling starts in ten minutes, and apparently we're all expected to participate."

"Caroling?" Brady groaned dramatically. "Every year she finds new ways to torture me."

"Oh, come on." Kimberly laughed. "It'll be fun. When's the last time you went caroling?"

"Exactly twelve months ago, the last time she roped me into it," Brady grumbled, but his tone was affectionate.

As the group began gathering their things, Lila found herself walking beside Sarah again. The afternoon had given her more questions than answers about Carol, but she felt closer to both Carol and Sarah in ways that surprised her.

"Thank you for today," she said to Sarah as they followed the others toward the caroling gathering point.

"For what?"

"For being such good company. For understanding why this season is hard. For just . . ." Lila struggled to find the right words. "For making me feel less alone."

Sarah's expression grew tender. "Oh, honey. You never have to thank me for caring about you. It's been my pleasure getting to know you."

The way Sarah said it, with such warmth and sincerity, made Lila's chest tighten with emotion. She'd come to Pine Ridge looking for one specific person from her past, but she was finding so much more than she'd expected.

As they joined the growing crowd around the gazebo in the town square, Lila caught sight of Carol organizing the sheet music and directing people into groups. The tree that would be lit tonight stood tall and dark in the center of the square, waiting for its moment to shine.

Tonight, Lila decided she would find a way to ask Carol more directly about her past. The festival had given her glimpses and hints, but she needed more concrete answers. She'd come too far to leave Pine Ridge without knowing the truth, and tomorrow was Christmas Eve, her intended departure date.

Sarah touched her arm gently. "Ready to make some questionable music with a bunch of strangers?"

"As ready as I'll ever be." Lila laughed, though her mind was already racing ahead to the evening's tree lighting ceremony.

One way or another, she was hoping tonight would bring her closer to the answers she'd come here to find.

Nine

The caroling group had assembled around the gazebo in the town square, a collection of familiar faces from the inn mixed with Pine Ridge locals bundled in winter coats and scarves. Carol stood at the front with a stack of song sheets, her cheeks pink from the cold and her eyes bright with excitement.

"All right, everyone," she called out, "we'll start with 'Silent Night' and work our way through the classics. Don't worry if you're not a singer. This is about spreading holiday cheer, not winning any competitions."

Brady appeared beside Lila, close enough that she could smell the faint scent of pine and soap that seemed to cling to him. "Fair warning," he said, his voice low and teasing, "I have been known to clear entire buildings with my singing."

"That bad?" Lila asked, surprised by his playful tone.

"Let's just say there's a reason I stick to chopping wood and fixing coffee machines." His eyes crinkled with humor. "What about you? Are you going to show us all up with your perfect pitch?"

"I wouldn't count on it. I'm more of a shower singer myself."

"You can hide in the back with me then," he said, grabbing her arm and leading her farther back in the crowd.

Lila's stomach fluttered both at his touch and the way he'd thawed toward her after their conversation the evening before. He wasn't the grump she'd taken him for at first, he was just guarded and protective of the inn and the couple who'd taken him in when he'd nearly lost it all.

By the time Carol got to them, she was down to one song sheet.

"We can share," he said, taking the paper. "As long as Lila doesn't tell me it would be faster to sing without the second round of the chorus." He flashed a smile at Lila.

She punched him playfully in the arm. "I'm not that bad."

Carol gave him a knowing smile, and Lila wondered if her instincts were right. Brady was flirting with her. It was probably just the lack of available women here around their age. The town's demographics trended a little older.

Brady had moved even closer now, holding the sheet up in front of them. The warmth radiating from his body made her acutely aware of his presence, and when his shoulder brushed hers as he leaned in to read the lyrics, she felt a chill run down her spine that had nothing to do with the winter air.

"Silent Night" began with Carol's clear soprano leading the way, and gradually other voices joined in. Brady, despite his warnings, had a pleasant baritone that blended nicely with the group. When Lila tentatively added her own voice to the mix, he glanced down at her, and she felt heat creep up her neck.

"Not bad," he murmured during a pause between verses.

"You too. You lied about the building-clearing thing."

"Maybe I just needed the right singing partner."

The comment, delivered with a small smile, made her stomach do a little flip. Was Brady Hanson actually charming behind those walls of his?

They moved through several more carols, their voices growing stronger and more confident as a group. During "Let it Snow," Brady caught her eye during the line about "the fire is slowly dying," and raised his eyebrows meaningfully toward the inn in the distance, where smoke was indeed rising from the chimney. She had to bite her lip to keep from laughing.

"You're taking this very literally," she whispered.

"I'm providing visual aids. It's educational." He flashed that smile again that threatened to buckle her knees.

Between songs, Lila watched Brady interact with the other carolers. He helped Mrs. Patterson, an elderly woman from town, adjust her scarf when the wind picked up. When a small boy tugged on his coat, Brady immediately crouched down to the child's eye level.

"Mr. Brady," the boy said, his words slightly muffled by his winter hat, "my mom says you know where Santa keeps his reindeer."

"Well," Brady said seriously, "that's classified information. But I might know someone who could arrange a special viewing." He glanced toward the boy's mother, who was watching with obvious affection. "If it's okay with your mom, you and I could take a walk tomorrow to see if we can spot any reindeer tracks in the snow behind the inn."

The child's eyes went wide with excitement. "Really?"

"Really. But it has to be early, before they fly back to the North Pole for their afternoon nap. They've got a big job to do tomorrow night."

Lila heart swelled as she watched Brady make promises to a little boy about imaginary reindeer tracks. The man who'd been so resistant to her suggestions about coffee machines was currently volunteering to wake up early on Christmas Eve morning to preserve a child's belief in magic. She'd been as wrong about him as he'd been about her.

"You're really something," she said quietly when Brady stood up.

"What do you mean?"

"That was incredibly sweet."

Brady's cheeks, already pink from the cold, seemed to redden further. "Kids should get to believe in magic, especially at Christmas."

Before Lila could respond, Carol was calling for their attention again. "All right, carolers, time for our grand finale. 'O Holy Night,' and then we'll head over to the tree lighting ceremony."

As the familiar melody began, Lila found herself standing closer to Brady than strictly necessary. His voice, rich and warm, seemed to wrap around hers as they sang together. When they reached the soaring high notes of "fall on your knees," she was surprised by the strength and beauty of his voice joining with the group.

"You really can sing," she said when the song ended to scattered applause from passersby.

"Only when properly motivated."

"What motivates you?"

Brady looked down at her, his green eyes serious despite the smile playing at his lips. "Good company."

The simple answer, delivered with quiet sincerity, made her breath catch. She didn't have time to be distracted from her mission in Pine Ridge, but Brady didn't feel strictly like a distraction. He was beginning to feel like an anchor. Like a safe harbor in uncertain winds.

The caroling group began dispersing, some heading home and others moving toward the town square where the tree lighting ceremony would begin shortly. Brady offered Lila his arm as they walked across the snowy street.

"Careful," he said, "it's getting slippery."

The gesture felt both practical and intimate, and Lila found herself enjoying the solid strength of his arm beneath her hand. They joined the growing crowd around the tall Christmas tree that dominated the town square, its dark branches outlined against the evening sky.

"How long have they been doing the tree lighting?" Lila asked as they found a spot with a good view.

"As long as I can remember. My parents used to bring me when I was little." Brady's voice grew softer. "It was always the highlight of Christmas for me, standing here with the whole town, watching the tree come to life."

"It must be bittersweet now, without them."

"Sometimes. But also comforting. Like when I'm somewhere we used to be together it's like they're here too, you know?"

Lila nodded in understanding. Her own parents had loved Christmas traditions, and she'd avoided them this year because they hurt too much. Maybe that had been the wrong approach though.

The crowd continued to grow as families with children, elderly couples, and groups of friends filled the square. Strings of lights had been strung between the lampposts, creating a magical canopy overhead. Vendors circulated through the crowd selling hot chocolate and roasted chestnuts, their calls adding to the festive atmosphere.

"Here," Brady said, pressing a steaming cup into her hands. "You looked cold."

"When did you—" She looked around, realizing he must have approached one of the vendors while she was distracted by the growing crowd. "Thank you."

"Can't have you freezing during the ceremony. That would be bad for Pine Ridge's reputation."

She took a sip of the hot chocolate, rich and warming, and caught Brady watching her reaction with obvious pleasure. "It's perfect." Although his small gesture made her feel warm in a way that had nothing to do with the hot chocolate.

A microphone crackled to life near the base of the tree, and Mayor Johnson stepped forward to address the crowd. After a few brief remarks about community and tradition, he introduced Carol as the evening's master of ceremonies.

"Carol Brennan has been the heart of our Christmas festival for more years than I can count," the mayor said. "She embodies the spirit of Pine Ridge—welcoming, generous, and dedicated to making everyone feel like family."

Carol looked radiant under the lights, her face glowing with genuine joy as she looked out over the crowd. When she began to speak, her voice carried clearly through the winter air.

"Thank you all for being here tonight," she began. "For thirty-eight years, I've had the privilege of calling Pine

Ridge home, and every year this ceremony reminds me of what makes this place so special.

"We gather here not just to light a tree, but to celebrate the connections that bind us together," Carol continued. "Pine Ridge is a family. We see each other through difficult times, and we celebrate each other's joys as if they were our own."

Brady moved slightly closer, and Lila was intensely aware of his presence beside her. His hand brushed against hers, and she had to fight to resist the urge to slip her hand into his.

"I've learned over the years that love multiplies when it's shared," Carol said, her voice carrying across the square. "The children we nurture, whether they're born to us or not." She made eye contact with Brady, and Lila looked over to see him give a small nod and smile in return. "The friends who become family. The strangers who become neighbors. Every act of kindness, every moment of connection, adds light to our community.

"And sometimes," Carol continued, her voice growing softer but somehow more powerful, "the most precious gifts are the ones we never expected to receive. The second chances, the new beginnings, and the new people who find their way to us through the most unexpected paths."

Lila felt tears prick her eyes. Whether Carol was her birth mother or not, the words felt like they were meant just for her.

"So tonight, as we light this tree together, let's remember that we're not just illuminating Pine Ridge. We're celebrating the light that each of us brings to this community, and the brightness we create when we choose to love one another."

The crowd erupted in applause, and Carol stepped back with a warm smile. The mayor returned to the microphone for the countdown, but Lila barely heard him. She didn't have to debate taking Brady's hand anymore, because Brady's hand had found hers, and when she looked up at him, she found him watching her with an expression that made her heart race.

"Ten . . . nine . . . eight . . ." the crowd chanted together.

"Seven . . . six . . . five . . ."

Brady leaned down, his voice low and meant only for her. "Are you okay?" He wiped a tear trickling down her cheek with a gloved finger.

"Four . . . three . . . two . . ."

"Happy tears," she whispered back.

"ONE!"

The tree burst to life in a cascade of golden lights, thousands of tiny bulbs transforming the dark evergreen into something magical. The crowd cheered and applauded, children squealed with delight, and someone began singing "O Christmas Tree."

But Lila barely noticed any of it. Brady was still looking at her with that intense, questioning expression, and she realized that somewhere between trying to rearrange the buffet, looking for the perfect tree, and Carol's speech about unexpected family, she'd started to fall for this man who fixed ancient coffee machines and promised little boys they'd see reindeer tracks.

"It truly is magical," Lila commented as she stared up in wonder at the lights twinkling on every branch.

Brady squeezed her hand. "It is," he said in a way that suggested he meant more than just the tree.

They stood there quietly as if they were the only two people in town, and it felt nice to be able to just be still with someone. Lila couldn't remember the last time she'd been able to just let herself be.

Someone from town stopped to tell Brady goodbye, and the spell was broken. The others from the inn had already begun walking back, and she could just make out their silhouettes down the street in the lamp light.

"We should probably head back," Brady said as the crowd thinned.

She nodded. "Probably."

He reached for her hand again, and they began walking slowly back toward the inn. The streets were quieter now, most of the festival activity winding down for the evening, but the whole town seemed to glow with the warmth of celebration and community.

Brady dropped her hand as they reached the front door of the inn, and she immediately missed the weight of it in hers. He must have seen the disappointment on her face.

"I need to go help Tom get a few things ready for tomorrow, but if you're not tired yet, maybe we could sit by the fire for a little while after?"

She nodded. "I'd like that. I'll just go change into something more comfortable."

"I'll meet you in the lobby in a half hour," he said.

As Lila climbed the stairs, she knew what she wanted to do. She was going to tell Brady why she'd really come to Pine Ridge. Maybe he knew something about Carol she didn't.

Ten

T hirty minutes later, Lila descended the stairs to find Brady carrying in more wood for the fire.

"I'm going to grab a cup of tea. Can I get you any?" Lila asked.

"Sure, I'll take a peppermint tea."

Lila made them each a tea over at the beverage station and resisted the urge to suggest they put a single-serve coffee maker that took both coffee and tea pods here like they had upstairs. It wasn't as flashy as the Brew Pro 11 she'd suggested a couple of days ago, but it would make tea a lot faster than the bag she was currently steeping in each cup. Maybe Brady had been right about slowing down though. The wait gave her time to plan what she was going to say to him.

Returning with two cups of tea in hand, Lila found Brady on the couch waiting for her.

"So did you enjoy your first Pine Ridge Christmas Festival?" he asked, accepting the tea she held out.

"Very much so," she said as she settled down next to him. "It must be really special growing up in a place like this."

"It was. The whole town was my family, even before I lost my own. Losing your parents is never easy, but I've never really felt alone here."

Lila nodded, wrapping her hands around her mug to keep them from shaking. She didn't feel alone here either, but she increasingly believed she did indeed have real family here too. And it was time to see if Brady might be able to help her uncover the truth.

"Brady," Lila said turning on the couch to face him, "if I tell you something important, can we keep it between us?"

He stopped and turned to face her, his expression growing serious. "Of course."

The firelight flickered across his face, illuminating his strong jaw and kind, perceptive eyes. A week ago, she would never have imagined trusting someone so completely. But somehow their connection had grown so much, she almost couldn't imagine not telling him.

"I want to tell you why I really came to Pine Ridge," she said, the words coming out in a rush before she could lose her nerve.

Brady's expression grew more attentive, but not worried. "Okay."

"It wasn't just for a quiet Christmas. I came here looking for someone." She paused, taking a deep breath. "I came to find my birth mother." The relief of finally saying it out loud was immediate and overwhelming. "I was adopted as a baby, and I had this clue—a quilt that led me here. I've been trying to figure out if she might still be in Pine Ridge."

Brady was quiet for a long moment, processing her words. "That's why you asked if I felt guilty about my relationship with the Brennans after my parents' death," he said, more as a statement than as a question.

"Yes. And Brady, I think—" She took a deep breath, knowing that once she said this, there would be no taking it back. "I think it might be Carol."

If she'd expected shock or disbelief, Brady surprised her. Instead, he just nodded slowly, as if the pieces of a puzzle were falling into place in his mind.

"That would explain a lot," he said quietly.

"You're not surprised?"

"I've watched you with her all week. There's something there, some kind of connection. And Carol . . ." He paused, seeming to choose his words carefully. "Carol has always carried a sadness about not having children. It's not something she's ever really talked about. I always thought she and Tom lost a baby. I never considered that perhaps she'd given one up for adoption. It must have been before she met Tom."

Lila felt tears burning her eyes and threatening to spill over. "So, you think it's possible?"

"I think," Brady said, reaching over to put his hand over hers, "that you being here, right now, isn't a coincidence. And I think whatever the truth is, we'll figure it out together."

The *we* in that sentence made her heart soar. "Really?"

"Really. Tell me what you know so far."

As she began to share everything she knew about her birth and the quilt, the weight she'd been carrying lifted ever so slightly now that she had someone to share it with. Brady's strong hand stayed on hers as she walked him through all the details of her adoption and her decision to come to Pine Ridge.

Brady was quiet for a long moment after Lila finished. The fire crackled softly between them, casting dancing shadows on the walls.

"So, this isn't just your first Christmas without either of your parents, it's also your first birthday without them," he said finally. "But now that they're gone, you've allowed yourself to wonder more about where you came from."

"Exactly. I've never known anything about the circumstances of my birth, just that it happened on Christmas and that someone cared enough to send a beautiful quilt with me." Lila's voice was barely above a whisper. "When I found out the quilt came from here, I had to come see for herself."

Brady leaned forward, his elbows on his knees as he studied her face in the firelight. "Tell me about the timing again. The quilt was delivered here on December 24th, 1991?"

"That's what Cynthia found in her mother's journal. A rush order completed and delivered to Pine Ridge Inn on Christmas Eve." Lila wrapped her hands more tightly around her mug. "I was born the next day."

"That fits," Brady said thoughtfully. "Carol came to Pine Ridge in her early twenties. She's told me before that she followed a man here. He had a job over at the ski resort in Breckenridge."

"That must be the 'bad boy' she mentioned to me earlier in the festival."

Brady nodded. "I've picked up bits and pieces over the years. She was involved with someone who wasn't good for her, someone who didn't stick around when things got difficult. Tom has hinted that the guy broke Carol's heart pretty badly."

"Do you think she could really be my birth mother? The baby ornament on the tree," Lila said, remembering Carol's reaction. "She got so emotional when Kimberly pulled it out of the box."

"And the way she talks about family—about how love multiplies when it's shared, about finding family in unexpected ways." Brady's voice grew more certain. "I always thought she was talking about me, about how they took me in. But maybe she was also talking about someone she had to let go."

The possibility hung between them, both hopeful and terrifying. Lila had spent the past couple of days wondering if Carol could be her birth mother, but hearing Brady confirm that it fit what he knew about Carol's past made it feel suddenly, dramatically real.

"What do I do now?" she asked. "I can't just walk up to her and ask if she gave birth to a baby thirty-four years ago."

Brady was quiet for a moment, then sat up straighter. "What if we could find some kind of confirmation first? Something that would give you more confidence before you approach her?"

"Like what?"

"Inn records. Guest registrations, birth certificates filed with the county, medical records . . . I don't know. Something that might document what happened here around Christmas 1991."

Lila shook her head. "My adoption was sealed, so there won't be any birth certificates or medical records we can access. Do you think Tom and Carol still have records from the inn that are that old?"

"Tom keeps everything. He's got boxes and boxes of old paperwork in the storage room behind the office. Financial records, guest registrations, correspondence—he says you never know when you might need something for tax purposes or insurance claims, and he likes to be able to go back if someone is a repeat visitor and check any notes on the activities they engaged in or food they enjoyed. Both Tom and his parents have always kept track of those things so they could tailor each guest's experience. Plus, we could go through the guests and at least figure out who was visiting that year at Christmas in case there are any other likely candidates."

"Would they let us look through them?"

Brady shrugged. "Technically, we don't need permission. I have access to all of that. It's not kept under lock and key or anything."

"When could we do that?"

Brady glanced toward the stairs, where the other guests had long since retired for the night. "Tonight? The other guests all seem to be in for the night, and Tom and Carol are already back at their cabin. We probably don't want to risk them coming back for something, finding us and asking questions, so let's wait a couple of hours. I know they like to be in bed by eleven."

"That feels so sneaky," Lila said, but even as she spoke, she knew it was what she needed to do.

"Looking at old records isn't going to hurt anyone. It'll just help us understand what we're dealing with."

Lila nodded slowly. The logic made sense, even if it made her stomach bubble with anxiety. "Okay. Let's do it."

"Are you sure? Once we start looking, we can't unknow whatever we find."

The question gave her pause. Was she ready for answers that might change everything? But then she thought about Carol's warmth, about the way she'd felt at home here from the moment she'd arrived, about the growing certainty that she was exactly where she needed to be.

"I'm sure," she said. "I came here for answers. I need to know the truth."

Brady smiled, and she felt a rush of gratitude for his steady presence, his willingness to help her navigate this uncertain territory. "Then we'll find them. Meet me down here at midnight?"

"Midnight," she agreed.

As they said goodbye for now and she headed upstairs, Lila felt a mixture of anticipation and terror. In a couple of hours, she might finally have the answers she'd come to Pine Ridge to find.

Lila lay in bed watching the red numbers on her alarm clock creep toward midnight. Every sound in the inn seemed amplified—the settling of old wood, the whisper of wind against her window, the distant hum of the heating system. Her heart hammered against her ribs as the minutes ticked by.

At 11:58, she slipped out of bed and pulled on leggings and an oversized sweatshirt. The hallway was dark and quiet, but she could see a sliver of light under Sarah's door. Everyone else seemed to be asleep.

She crept down the stairs, trying to avoid the steps she'd noticed creaked during her earlier trips up and down. The lobby was lit only by the dying embers in the fireplace, casting everything in a warm orange glow.

Brady was already there, sitting in one of the armchairs by the fire. He looked up as she approached, his expression both serious and reassuring.

"Ready?" he whispered.

She nodded, not trusting her voice.

They made their way to the small office behind the front desk, Brady producing a key from his pocket.

Brady flipped on the light, shutting the door behind them. The storage space was cramped but organized, with metal shelving lined with banker's boxes labeled with years and categories.

"Here," he said quietly, pointing to a section of boxes marked with years from the late 1980s through the mid-1990s. "Guest registrations are separate from financial records."

They carefully lifted down the box marked "Guest Records 1990–1992" and carried it over to a table. Inside the box, manila folders were organized chronologically, each containing registration forms, correspondence, and notes about individual guests. Lila's hands trembled slightly as she began flipping through them.

"December 1991," she murmured, searching through the folders. "October, November . . . wait."

She paused, staring at the filing tabs. November 1991 was there, but the next folder was February 1992.

"Brady," she whispered, her voice tight with disappointment. "December 1991 is missing."

He leaned over her shoulder to look at the files. "That's unusual. Tom is incredibly methodical about record-keeping."

They searched through the entire box, checking to see if the December folder had been misfiled elsewhere. But there was no trace of any records from December 1991.

"It's not here," Lila said, sinking back in the office chair. "The one month I need, and it's completely gone."

Lila felt tears pricking her eyes as frustration and uncertainty mixed together. She'd been so close to finding concrete evidence, only to hit another dead end.

"What do I do now?" she asked, her voice barely audible. "I feel like I'm trying to catch a shadow."

Brady reached over and took her hand. "You could ask Carol. Tell her why you're here and what you suspect. Maybe it's time for an honest conversation."

"What if I'm wrong? Or what if she doesn't want to know me? She did seal the adoption. What if I ruin whatever connection we've built this week?"

"Or what if," Brady said softly, "she's been hoping for thirty-four years that you'd find your way back to her?"

The possibility made Lila's chest tighten with a mixture of hope and terror. "Do you really think that's possible?"

"I think Carol Brennan has one of the biggest hearts of anyone I've ever known. And I think if she gave up a child once, it was because she thought it was best for that child, not because she didn't love them. Look, Lila, I wouldn't encourage you to do this if I thought it was a bad idea. Carol means a lot to me too."

Lila wiped tears from her cheeks, feeling something shift inside her. "I'm supposed to leave tomorrow," she said. "I was planning to spend Christmas at home."

"So stay. Christmas kind of seems like the perfect time for this conversation, don't you think? Besides, no one should be alone on Christmas or their birthday, and definitely not when they fall on the same day."

She looked at Brady's face in the lamplight, at his kind eyes and encouraging expression, and felt a surge of gratitude for this man who'd become so much more than she'd expected when she arrived in Pine Ridge.

"Would you be there with me? When I talk to her?"

"If you want me there, I'll be there." His voice was resolute with solidarity.

They carefully returned the box to its place on the storage room shelf, erasing any evidence of their midnight search. As they prepared to return to their respective beds, Lila felt simultaneously exhausted and energized. She still didn't have definitive proof, but she had something else now—the certainty that she was going to see this through to the end.

"Thank you," she whispered as they reached the bottom of the stairs. "For . . . everything."

Brady reached for her hand and squeezed it. "Get some sleep. Tomorrow's going to be a big day."

As Lila climbed the stairs to her room, she felt a mixture of anticipation and terror about what Christmas Eve might bring. But for the first time since arriving in Pine Ridge, she wasn't facing the unknown alone.

In the morning, she would extend her stay. And then, when the moment felt right, she would ask Carol Brennan the question that had brought her to Pine Ridge: Are you my mother?

Eleven

Lila woke on Christmas Eve morning with sunlight streaming through her window and the sound of voices drifting up from the lobby below. For a moment, she lay still, remembering everything that had happened the night before—the tree lighting ceremony, her confession to Brady, their midnight search through the inn's records, and most importantly, her decision to stay through Christmas.

Today was supposed to be her departure day. She'd originally planned to be on the road by now, driving back to her empty condo to spend Christmas and her birthday alone. Instead, she was about to extend her stay and potentially change everything.

Lila pushed back curtains and peered out her bedroom window, squinting through the early morning light to see if more snow had fallen overnight. Instead, she saw Brady crouched near the big oak tree by the front porch, doing something in the snow that she couldn't quite make out.

What was he doing out there so early?

Brady moved methodically around the yard, occasionally glancing toward the driveway. He had something in his hand, but from this angle she couldn't tell what it was. Every few steps, he'd stop and press whatever it was into the snow, then move on.

A car pulled into the circular drive, and Brady straightened, throwing whatever had been in his hand behind a tree and brushing snow off his gloves. A woman climbed out of the passenger side, followed by a small boy who immediately started bouncing on his toes despite the cold.

Understanding dawned as she recognized the little boy. Reindeer tracks. Brady was making reindeer tracks for the little boy from the festival.

Lila smiled, pulling on warm layers. When she found Sarah in the coffee nook, she told her she had to come outside with her to see something.

They shrugged on their winter coats, slipped on gloves, and made their way out onto the porch. The cold air hit Lila's face and she pulled the hood of her coat over her head, taking a sip of the coffee she'd grabbed, hoping it would warm her from within.

"Do you really think they came here?" The child's excited voice carried across the snowy yard.

"Well," Brady said, his voice taking on the same serious tone she'd heard him use with the other children at the festival, "I did see some unusual tracks this morning. Want to help me investigate?"

The little boy nodded so vigorously his winter hat slipped over his eyes. His mother laughed and adjusted it, mouthing "thank you" to Brady over her son's head.

"What are they doing?" Sarah asked, confused.

"Brady put reindeer tracks in the snow for the kid to find. He told him a story last night at the festival about how the reindeer hang out here before they head to the North Pole this afternoon to help Santa."

Sarah smiled. "Well, isn't that just delightful." She followed Lila over to where two rocking chairs sat nearby.

Lila settled into one of the rockers, passing Sarah one of the two heavy blankets she'd taken from the basket near the door. Cradling her mug, she watched as Brady lead the child around the yard, pointing out each carefully placed hoofprint. The boy's delighted shrieks pierced the quiet morning as he discovered track after track, his mitten-covered hands gesturing wildly as he explained to his mother how Rudolph must have stopped for a snack from the oak tree.

"And look, Mom! Look! They went toward the barn!" The boy took off running, following Brady's carefully planted trail. "I bet they're still there!"

Brady caught Lila's eye on the porch and gave her a little wave as his now familiar slow smile spread across his face, making her stomach do little flips. She lifted her coffee mug in a small salute.

"I see you two have finally become friends," Sarah said, raising an eyebrow.

Lila's cheeks flushed despite the cold winter air. "Something like that."

"His charm is hard to resist," Sarah said with obvious affection. "When he was a younger man, he brought a woman to the festivities here a time or two, but I'm not sure he's ever really gotten serious with anyone. He's a thoughtful man, but he's doesn't seem to allow himself to get too close to anyone. Of course, I'm one to talk. I never really had eyes for anyone after my David."

Lila hadn't really let anyone get close in a long time either. It was a mixture of a bad breakup a few years earlier and her dedication to her work. Then her dad had gotten sick, and she'd spent all her free time in Atlanta with her mom. And then, well, she'd ended up here.

"What about you?" Sarah asked, turning to her. "Do you have someone back home?"

She shook her head. "No, it's been a while."

"Well, there's nothing quite so romantic as Christmastime, don't you think?" Sarah said, her eyes twinkling as she looked over at Lila and then out to where Brady had walked across the yard with the little boy.

Lila watched as he kneeled so he was eye level with the kid, pointing toward the tree line where the tracks led deeper into the woods. The boy listened with rapt attention, his face glowing with wonder.

She wasn't a grinch, but she did feel her heart grow two sizes—just like Tom's depiction in charades—as she watched Brady high-five the little boy, then follow as the boy ran toward the trees. It wasn't exactly romance Lila was looking for, but it had been nice to share her burden with Brady the night before. And he certainly was easy to look at, especially now that he wasn't scowling at her and her suggestions anymore.

The group hunting for reindeer tracks had disappeared around the back of the inn, so Lila suggested they go in to warm up. The lobby was bustling with the usual morning activity. Sophie and Miles were warming their hands by the fire, the sisters were planning their day over coffee, and Ali and Mike were bundled up for another day of skiing.

Carol emerged from the kitchen carrying a fresh pot of coffee, her face lighting up when she saw Lila.

"Good morning, dear. I was just thinking about you." Carol's smile was warm but held a hint of curiosity. "Are you already packing your car? I hope you're not rushing off too early. The roads can be tricky this time of morning."

This was it. Lila took a deep breath, feeling Brady's encouraging words from the night before echo in her mind.

"Actually, Carol, I was hoping I could extend my stay through Christmas. I know it's last minute, but—"

"Of course!" Carol's face broke into a genuine smile that seemed to illuminate her entire being. "I'm so pleased. Christmas Day just wouldn't be the same without you here with us." She paused, her expression growing softer. "I had a feeling you might decide to stay. I'm so pleased we've won you over."

"Thank you," Lila said, relief flooding through her. "I just realized I wasn't ready to leave yet."

"If you think the last few days have been fun, just wait until you see what we have in store tonight and tomorrow," Carol said, patting Lila's arm gently. "You're part of our little Christmas family now."

The words made Lila's chest tighten with emotion. A quiet "Thank you," was all she could manage.

Before Carol could respond, Sarah appeared at Lila's elbow having refilled her mug with coffee.

"Did I hear you say you're staying through Christmas?" Sarah asked, her eyes twinkling with pleasure. "That's wonderful news. I was hoping you would."

"Were you?"

"Of course." Sarah's eyes narrowed. "I suspected you were going home to spend Christmas alone, and I couldn't bear the thought of that."

Lila was surprised Sarah had discovered her plan. She had tried to make it sound to everyone like she had big plans, being vague so she wasn't outright lying to them. "How did you know?"

"Just intuition," Sarah said, putting an arm around Lila to squeeze her. "The holidays are for sharing with others." Sarah's voice was gentle but certain. "And sometimes Christmas has a way of bringing together just the right people to make it special."

Lila studied Sarah's face, struck by the warmth in her expression. There was something about the way Sarah looked at her that reminded her of her mother, and she realized there was nothing she wanted more than to spend Christmas with these people who really had begun to feel like family in just the few days she'd spent in Pine Ridge.

"Would you like to take a walk with me after breakfast?" Sarah asked. "I always enjoy a quiet stroll on Christmas Eve morning. There's something peaceful about the town before all the day's festivities begin."

An hour later, Lila and Sarah were bundled in their winter coats, walking slowly down Main Street. The town was quieter than it had been during the festival, most shops closed for the holiday, but the Christmas decorations seemed even more magical in the soft morning light without the distraction of the crowd and the booths.

"It's beautiful," Lila said, breathing in the crisp air. "I can see why you keep coming back here."

"Pine Ridge has always felt like home to me," Sarah said, her voice thoughtful. "More so than anywhere I've lived, actually. I think I fell in love with Pine Ridge the way you fall in love with a person. I miss it when I'm away."

"Have you ever thought about moving to Pine Ridge permanently?" Lila asked as they sat on a bench in front of the big Christmas tree they'd watch light the previous evening. "You clearly love it here, and it seems like it would be a peaceful place to live year-round."

Sarah was quiet for a moment, her eyes fixed on the tree. "I've thought about it," she admitted. "More than once, actually. It's like there's a piece of me here, and the closest I feel to being complete is when I'm here."

"So, what's stopping you from moving here?"

"At first, it was because I was caring for my mother, but she passed a few years back. Then it was my job I couldn't imagine leaving. I'm a counselor at an elementary school." Sarah's voice grew warm with obvious affection for her work. "There's something about helping kids navigate difficult times, being there when they need someone to listen . . . It feels like the most important thing I could be doing with my life. I've watched for openings at the schools near here, but nothing yet. Maybe one day."

"Your work sounds incredibly rewarding," Lila said, touched by the passion in Sarah's voice.

"It is. These kids, some of them are dealing with things no child should have to face. Divorce, loss, feeling like they don't belong anywhere." Sarah's expression grew tender. "When I can help even one child feel less alone in the world, then I feel less alone too."

"How long have you been doing that kind of work?"

"Pretty much my whole career. I started in social work right after college, but I found my calling working directly with children a few years after David passed. There's something about being able to make a difference in a young person's life, to help them believe they're worthy of love and care . . ." Sarah trailed off, her voice thick with emotion.

Lila was struck by the intensity of Sarah's commitment to her work with children. "It sounds like more than just a job for you."

"It is," Sarah said softly. "I suppose you could say it's my way of trying to make the world a little better, one child at a time. Sometimes I think about all the children out there who need someone in their corner, and I can't imagine walking away from that responsibility."

They sat quietly for a moment, both lost in their own thoughts about purpose and duty and the complicated ways love shapes our choices. Lila found herself admiring Sarah's dedication, the way she'd built her life around helping vulnerable children.

"Those kids are lucky to have you," Lila said finally.

Sarah's smile was warm but carried a hint of something deeper. "I hope so. I've made mistakes in my life, and I know I'm not perfect, but I hope my work with them has atoned for some of my shortcomings and mistakes."

They walked in comfortable silence for a few minutes, their footsteps crunching softly in the snow. When they reached the last building on Main Street, Sarah paused before they turned to retrace their steps.

"You know," Sarah said, "I've been thinking about what you said yesterday about losing your mother this past spring."

Lila's chest tightened slightly. "It's still hard to believe she's gone sometimes."

"The first Christmas without someone you love is always the most difficult," Sarah said gently. "What was she like? Your mother?"

"She was . . . everything to me," Lila said, surprised by how easily the words came. "Patient, kind, always knew exactly what to say when I was struggling. She had this way of making even ordinary moments feel special. Christmas was her absolute favorite time of year."

Sarah's expression grew tender. "She sounds wonderful. I bet she would have loved seeing you here, experiencing a Pine Ridge Christmas."

"She would have," Lila agreed, feeling tears prick her eyes. "She always said the holidays were about making memories with people you love, not about fancy decorations or expensive gifts."

"Wise woman," Sarah said softly. "My mother was like that too. I still find myself wanting to call her whenever something beautiful happens, like last night's tree lighting."

As they walked quietly, Lila thought about mothers and how they shaped children into the people they became. Sometimes it was for the better, sometimes for the worse.

And, in her case, how they also shaped their children by the decisions they made.

Back at the inn, they found Brady in the lobby talking to Tom about something involving horses and saddles.

"Perfect timing," Brady said when he saw Lila. "We were just talking about taking some of the horses out this afternoon to see some of the countryside around Pine Ridge."

"Horseback riding?" Lila asked, surprised.

"Nothing too adventurous," Brady assured her. "Sarah, what do you say?"

Sarah shook her head. "Not me. I just got to the good part of my book, so I want to sit by the fire and finish it today."

"Sophie and Miles already passed," Tom said, "but Carol went to see if Kimberly and Kendall want to join us."

"I haven't been horseback riding since I was a kid," Lila admitted. She was nervous about embarrassing herself out there, but a horseback ride through the snow did sound magical.

"We'll put you on Thunder." He smiled when he saw the look on Lila's face at the horse's name. "Despite his name, Thunder is as gentle as a lamb," he assured her.

"Thunder will take good care of you," Tom said with a grin. "He's been giving gentle trail rides for years. And Brady knows those trails better than anyone."

Carol returned without Kimberly or Kendall. "The ladies are staying in to watch Christmas movies all day. Apparently, that's a big tradition in their household."

"I think it's just the four of us then," Tom said.

Carol looked between Brady and Lila. "You know what, we should probably stay back and start prepping our big dinner, so it'll be ready when we all return from the Christmas Eve service."

Tom started to protest, but Carol gave him a look and Lila realized Carol was intentionally sending her and

Brady off alone. Apparently, Sarah wasn't the only one who'd picked up on their growing connection.

"You're right, dear," Tom said. "Lead the way."

"Guess it's just the two of us," Brady said. "It'll be like getting your own private lesson."

Lila debated staying back to confront Carol, but she wasn't ready yet. Taking the horses out might be just what she needed to spend her nervous energy.

"When were you thinking?" Lila asked Brady.

"How about noon? I'll pack some sandwiches. That should give us plenty of time before we need to be back for the Christmas Eve service."

"It's a date," Lila said, then felt heat rise to her cheeks at her inadvertent choice of words.

Brady's smile suggested he didn't mind the slip. "It's a date."

Two hours later, Lila found herself following Brady toward a small stable behind the inn. She was bundled in her warmest clothes, her nervousness about both the horseback riding and the conversation she needed to have later with Carol making her stomach churn.

"Tom's grandfather built this stable when horses were still the primary way to get around these mountains," Brady explained as he led a gentle-looking chestnut horse out of one of the stalls. "We don't keep many horses anymore, but Thunder and Buttercup both love a good trail ride."

"Wait," Lila teased, "you're getting Buttercup and I'm getting Thunder? A horse named Buttercup sounds more my speed."

Brady laughed. "You wouldn't say that if you knew her. Trust me on this one. Let's just say Buttercup has a mind of her own sometimes, but she seems to be partial to me."

"So, you have a way with all the ladies then, even the four-legged ones?" Lila smiled at him.

"Yes, but I prefer the two-legged ones with blonde hair, brown eyes, and lots of suggestions about efficiency and organization," he said, a twinkle of mischief in his eyes.

Lila felt her cheeks blush and hoped he didn't notice because they were probably already pink from the cold air. Brady wasn't even trying to hide his flirting anymore. Not that she minded. It was a pleasant distraction from her real mission in Pine Ridge.

Thunder was indeed gentle, standing patiently as Brady helped Lila into the saddle and adjusted her stirrups. When he held her hand to help her up, she tried to concentrate on swinging her leg over the saddle and not the way electricity shot up her arm from his touch.

Brady mounted Buttercup—which he told her was a palomino with its dark gold coat and white-blonde hair—with the easy confidence of someone who'd been riding his whole life.

"Just relax and let him do the work," Brady said as they started down a trail that wound through the trees behind the inn. "Thunder knows this route by heart."

The first few minutes were nerve-wracking as Lila adjusted to the rhythm of the horse's gait, but gradually she began to relax and enjoy the experience. The trail led them through snow-covered evergreens, the silence broken only by the soft sound of hoofbeats and the occasional call of a winter bird.

"This is incredible," she said as they emerged from the trees onto a ridge that offered a spectacular view of the valley below. Pine Ridge looked like a miniature Christmas village nestled among the mountains, smoke rising from chimneys and the distant sparkle of the big tree in the town square visible even in daylight.

"It's my favorite place to come when I need to think," Brady said, dismounting and moving to help her down from Thunder's back. "There's something about being up here that puts everything in perspective."

They tied the horses to a sturdy pine tree and found a fallen log where Brady placed a thick blanket for them to sit. It offered a perfect seat overlooking the valley. Brady pulled drinks and sandwiches from the bag he'd brought along, handing one of each to her.

"So," he said, settling beside her close enough that their shoulders touched, "how are you feeling about your decision to stay?"

"Terrified," Lila admitted. "But also certain that it's what I need to do. After last night, I knew I couldn't leave without knowing the truth. But what if I'm wrong about them? What if I came all this way and built up all these hopes for nothing?"

Brady turned to face her more fully, his green eyes serious. "Then you still found something valuable here. You found a place where you feel like you belong, people who care about you, and experiences that have changed you." He gave her a teasing smile. "And you found me, without whom this entire experience would be less memorable."

She laughed. "Fair enough."

As they ate their lunch, he told her about growing up in Pine Ridge. It sounded like he'd only spent time indoors long enough to sleep. He hiked, snowboarded, kayaked, went fly fishing, and whitewater rafting.

"It's why the job at the inn is perfect for me. I get to take guests to do all those things and call it work."

"I know what you mean," she said. "I get to book spa treatments and fancy dinner reservations at the hotels where I work so I can offer suggestions for improvements. It's definitely the best part of what I do."

"And do the managers always get grumpy about your suggestions?"

She smiled, shaking her head. "No, they're usually owned by corporations, not individuals, so it's a little less personal. The management track at the big resorts tends to be such that people move around a lot."

"So how are you enjoying the personal touch here in Pine Ridge?" He gestured at the landscape before them, obviously proud of himself for treating her to a fun afternoon.

"More than I thought I would," she admitted, bumping her shoulder against his playfully.

They were quiet for a moment as they took in the scenery. As she watched the smoke puff from the chimney of the inn down below, she was curious if Brady would one day take over the inn, so she asked him.

"We've talked about it," he said. "Tom and Carol would like to start traveling more, especially during the quieter times of the year, so I've started taking over more of the back office work already. I was always afraid they might sell since they didn't have children to leave it to . . ." His voice trailed off, no doubt remembering their conversation from the previous evening.

Would things change if she was indeed Carol's daughter? It was a ridiculous thing to even think about right now. Even if she was, Brady was the person who deserved to inherit the inn. He was the one they'd actually helped raise. And besides, she couldn't get ahead of herself.

"Don't look at me," she said, holding up a hand and laughing. "I'm not trying to home in on your inheritance."

"Good." He smiled at her. "Because we aren't getting that Brew Pro whatever you want. I'm sure it would take a degree in electrical engineering to fix that thing."

"You know," she teased, "that's what extended warranties are for."

"You just like to spend other people's money, don't you?"

She shrugged. "It is actually kind of fun."

"Well, this place can't afford someone like you."

"Oh, I'd write up a plan for this place for free if I thought you'd actually follow it."

"But you know better, right?"

"I do. You're a lost cause."

"Or maybe just not properly motivated," he challenged, wiggling his eyebrows.

"Okay, Romeo," she said, playfully punching his arm. "We better get back so we can clean up for this big Christmas Eve feast Carol promised."

"I'm wearing you down," he said as he gathered up the trash from their lunch and stuffed it back in his bag. "You're almost having fun."

"I *am* having fun," she assured him. "Thank you for helping get my mind off things."

"Of course," he said, untying Thunder from where he was secured to a tree.

Now that it was time to head back, the conversation Lila needed to have with the woman she thought might be her birth mother occupied her thoughts.

"Any advice on how to approach Carol?" Lila asked him.

"Follow your instincts. You'll know when the moment is right." Brady helped her back up onto Thunder, his hands lingering at her waist for just a moment longer than necessary. She missed his touch the instant it was gone. "And remember, whatever happens, Carol is a good person. If she is your birth mother, any pain or surprise will come from a place of love, not rejection. Remember that you've had more time to process this than she has."

The ride back to the inn felt shorter than the ride out, perhaps because Lila was more comfortable in the saddle now, or perhaps because she was dreading the end of this peaceful interlude. As they approached the stable, she could see warm light pouring from nearly every window of the inn, the lights wound around the porch railing adding a festive glow.

Inside, the lobby buzzed with Christmas Eve preparations. Sophie and Miles were stringing popcorn for the tree, the sisters were arranging evergreen boughs on the mantel, and Sarah was polishing silver candlesticks at the dining room table. The scene was so picture-perfect, so full of warmth and tradition, that Lila felt a pang of longing for all the Christmases spent at her childhood home.

Carol appeared from the kitchen, wiping her hands on an apron decorated with holly and berries. "How was your ride?" she asked, her face glowing with the pleasure of someone who loved seeing others enjoy themselves.

"Magical," Lila said, meaning it. "The town looks so beautiful from up there."

"Yes, it's beautiful this time of year," Carol agreed. "I'm so glad you got to see it. Now, I hope you both worked up an appetite, because we're planning quite a feast for tonight."

"Is there anything I can help with after I get cleaned up?" Lila asked.

"Sarah's been such a dear, helping all afternoon," Carol said, gesturing toward the dining room where Sarah was now setting the table. "But if you'd like to help me with the final touches in the kitchen in about an hour, I'd welcome the company."

An hour later, they were working side by side, adding garnishes to platters and arranging rolls in baskets. Lila found herself studying Carol again. When Carol hummed softly while she worked, Lila wondered if she'd inherited her love of music from this woman. When Carol adjusted a flower arrangement with careful precision, Lila thought about her own eye for design and detail.

"Carol," she began, then stopped, not sure how to continue.

"Yes, dear?"

"I just wanted to say how grateful I am that you let me extend my stay. This place, being here with all of you . . . it's exactly what I needed this Christmas."

Carol's expression softened, and she reached over to squeeze Lila's hand. "You know, Lila, from the moment you arrived, I've felt like you belonged here. There's something about you that just fits with our little family."

The words hung in the air between them, heavy with possibility and unspoken questions. Lila felt like they were dancing around the edges of something enormous, both of them perhaps sensing a connection they couldn't quite name.

"Sometimes," Carol continued, her voice growing thoughtful, "I think the people who are meant to be in our lives just find their way to us, as if by magic. In this case, a little Christmas magic, I suppose."

Before Lila could respond, Brady appeared in the kitchen doorway. "Ladies, Tom's calling for all hands in the dining room. Apparently, there's some debate about proper candle placement that requires a committee decision."

The moment broke, but as they made their way to the dining room, Lila caught Carol watching her with an expression she couldn't quite read. Tonight, during Christmas Eve dinner, she was going to find the courage to ask the question that had brought her to Pine Ridge. Whether Carol was her birth mother or not, she needed to know the truth.

As she helped carry the final dishes to the dining room, where the rest of their Christmas Eve family was gathering around the candlelit table, Lila felt a mixture of anticipation and peace. Whatever happened next, she was exactly where she wanted to be this Christmas Eve.

Twelve

After a lovely five o'clock Christmas Eve service at the church in town, the group walked the short distance back to the inn for the big dinner Carol and Tom had planned. The table had been set before they left, and all that was left was to take the food out of the warming oven.

The dining room glowed with candlelight as the group gathered around the long farmhouse table for Christmas Eve dinner. Carol had outdone herself with the traditional feast—roasted turkey with herb stuffing, a baked ham, roasted vegetables that smelled of rosemary and thyme, and fresh cranberry sauce in cut crystal bowls that sparkled from the flame of the candle nearby. Formal china was set at each place, and fresh evergreen boughs wound down the center of the table, scenting the air with the smell of Christmas.

"This is absolutely beautiful, Carol," Sophie said, settling into her chair beside Miles. "I can't remember the last time I didn't have to slave over a stove making a holiday meal."

"You've really outdone yourself," agreed Kendall, admiring the elegant table setting. "This is even nicer than dining in a fancy restaurant."

Carol beamed with pleasure as she took her seat at the head of the table. "Christmas Eve dinner has always been special to me. There's something magical about gathering with people you care about on this particular night."

Tom stood to pour wine while Brady helped carry the last few dishes from the kitchen. The conversation flowed easily as platters were passed and plates filled. Lila found herself between Sarah and Brady, feeling surrounded by warmth and belonging in a way that made her chest tight with emotion.

"So, what's everyone's favorite Christmas tradition?" Kimberly asked as she spooned stuffing onto her plate. "Besides amazing dinners like this, of course."

"Miles and I always open one present on Christmas Eve," Sophie said. "Something small, usually new pajamas or slippers. It started when our kids were little, and we needed something to tide them over until morning."

"We do breakfast for dinner on Christmas Eve," Kendall added. "Pancakes, eggs, bacon, biscuits—it's a feast. It's completely different from this, but there's something about breaking the rules on Christmas that makes it feel extra special."

"What about you, Sarah?" Kimberly asked. "Any special traditions?"

Sarah's fork paused halfway to her mouth. "This?" Sophie and Carol both laughed. "I can't even remember what I did before I started spending my Christmases here."

Just as Brady was asking Tom about how his parents had handled Christmas celebrations at the inn when he was growing up, Ali's phone rang where she had it face down on the table next to her plate. She flipped it over and glanced at the screen with a frown.

"It's my sister," she said apologetically. "She's pregnant and not due for another three weeks but let me just make sure everything's okay."

Ali answered the phone, moving slightly away from the table. The rest of them continued their conversation, but Lila noticed how Ali's expression changed from casual concern to excitement mixed with panic.

"Oh my God, seriously? Right now?" Ali was saying. "But you're not supposed to—okay, okay, I'll look at flights. I love you, and I'll be praying for the healthy arrival of my beautiful niece."

She hung up and turned back to the table, her face breaking into a broad smile. "My sister just went into labor a month early. She's at the hospital right now."

"How exciting!" Kendall exclaimed. "Are you getting a niece or a nephew?"

"Yes, she's having a little girl," Ali said, sinking back into her chair. "I can't believe it's happening on Christmas Eve. Mike, we need to see if we can change our flight and head back tomorrow."

"Of course," Mike said immediately, already pulling out his phone. "Let me check what's available."

The table erupted with congratulations and concerned questions about the baby and Ali's sister. While Mike worked on finding flights, the group rallied around Ali with support and excitement.

"A Christmas baby," Carol said, her voice soft with wonder. "How magical."

Something about Carol's tone, combined with the co-incidence of a baby being born on Christmas Eve, or maybe even Christmas Day if labor took a while, triggered a decision in Lila that surprised her. She felt Brady's eyes on her and realized this was the opening she'd been waiting for.

"You know," Lila said, her voice carrying over the conversation, "I'm actually a Christmas baby myself."

"Really?" Kimberly said. "How fun! Your birthday is tomorrow?"

"Christmas Day," Lila confirmed, her heart hammering against her ribs. Next to her, Brady put a supportive hand on her knee.

"That must make Christmas extra special for you," Miles said warmly.

Lila took a deep breath, knowing this was her moment. "It's always been a little complicated, actually. I was adopted as a baby, so I've never known much about the circumstances of my birth."

Carol's fork clattered against her plate, and Sarah coughed as she choked on her wine next to Lila.

"In fact," she glanced at Brady, who gave her a reassuring nod, "it's why I came to Pine Ridge this Christmas. I discovered that the quilt my birth mother sent with me was made by Emily, who owned the quilt shop on Main Street. So, I thought maybe I could find answers about where I came from here."

As Kimberly, Kendall, and Ali all spoke at once with excited, "Omigosh, really?", "That's crazy!", and "That's incredible!", Carol stood abruptly, her chair scraping against the hardwood floor.

"I'm sorry, I just need to check on the dessert," Carol said, her voice tight with emotion.

"I'll help you," Sarah said immediately, rising from her chair. "That's a lot of dishes to manage alone."

They disappeared into the kitchen together, leaving the rest of the table in slightly awkward silence. Brady reached for Lila's hand and squeezed it gently. She wondered if she should follow them into the kitchen, but she didn't want to confront Carol about her suspicions in front of Sarah. Based on her reaction though, Lila was even more sure she was on the right track.

"That's incredible that you traced the quilt here to Pine Ridge," Sophie said. "Have you ever tried to search for information about your birth family before?"

"Not until recently," Lila admitted. "Losing my parents made me realize how important family connections are, and I started wondering more about the people I came from."

"I got a flight," Mike announced, looking up from his phone. "Well, Christmas night. Nothing available before then, but we'll be able to make it back late that evening."

"I guess that'll have to do," Ali said. "We can keep checking in case anyone cancels and opens up seats."

In the kitchen, Lila could hear the murmur of voices but couldn't make out specific words. Carol and Sarah had been in there for several minutes now, longer than it would take to simply check on dessert. It seemed like Sarah had followed Carol to offer support after her obvious distress over Lila's revelation.

"I assume you asked Cynthia about the quilt?" Sophie asked.

"I did, but she didn't have much to go on," Lila said, intentionally leaving out that it had been delivered to the inn. There was no need to expose Carol to everyone else.

When Carol and Sarah finally returned, they were each carrying a pie, and Carol had a pot of coffee in her other hand. Carol's composure seemed restored, but both her and Sarah's eyes were slightly red.

"I hope everyone saved room for dessert," Carol said with forced cheer. "We've got a sweet potato pie and a pumpkin pie."

As they served the pie and passed around coffee, the conversation gradually returned to lighter topics. Ali shared more details about her sister's pregnancy, the sisters debated whether the new baby would be spoiled by having a Christmas birthday, asking Lila whether she hated having her birthday presents wrapped in Christmas paper—she did—and Tom told stories about other memorable Christmas Eve dinners at the inn.

But Lila noticed how Carol kept glancing at her when she thought no one was looking, and how Sarah seemed to be keeping a close eye on Carol as well.

"This has been the most wonderful Christmas Eve dinner," Sophie said as the meal wound down. "Thank you, Carol and Tom, for making it so special."

"It's been my pleasure," Carol replied, but her smile seemed fragile. "Having all of you here sharing stories and traditions, it's what Christmas is all about."

As the group began clearing dishes and preparing for the evening's sleigh ride, Lila caught Carol studying her face with an intensity that made her stomach flutter. Tomorrow was Christmas Day—her birthday—and somehow she knew that everything would change.

Brady appeared at her elbow as she carried plates to the kitchen. "How are you feeling?" he asked quietly.

"Like I just lit a fuse and now I'm waiting for the explosion," she admitted.

As the rest of the group prepared to bundle up for the traditional Christmas Eve sleigh ride, Lila could see Carol and Sarah standing close together as they cleared the dining room table of dishes, their heads bent in quiet conversation.

"It's a beautiful night for a sleigh ride," Brady said softly, his hand briefly touching her back in a gesture of support. "Whatever the truth is, we'll face it tomorrow."

Lila felt a mixture of anticipation and terror about what Christmas Day might bring. She'd come to Pine Ridge looking for answers about her past, but she was beginning to realize she might be about to discover so much more than she'd ever expected.

Twenty minutes later, they were all gathered in the lobby in their warmest coats and scarves. Tom had hitched the sleigh to Thunder and Buttercup, whose breath Lila could see through the window creating small clouds in the crisp night air.

"The sleigh only holds two at a time," Tom announced, "so we'll do four trips. Just a quick ride up and down Main Street since it's so cold. Who wants to go first?"

"We will, if that's okay," Ali said immediately, taking Mike's arm. "I want to get back and call my mom for an update on my sister."

Lila watched as they settled into the sleigh under thick wool blankets, and Tom guided the horses away into the snowy night.

"We can go next," Sophie said when Tom returned, and Miles helped her down the porch steps toward the sleigh.

When the older couple returned from their trip down Main Street, the sisters claimed the third ride.

"I guess that just leaves us," Lila said to Sarah, who had just returned from cleaning up the dining room with Carol.

Sarah shook her head with an apologetic smile. "Actually, I think it's too cold for me, and I've done it so many times before. Would you mind if I stayed back and helped Carol get the breakfast casseroles ready?" She looked to Brady with a knowing look. "I bet Brady here would take a ride with you."

"Sure. We can let Tom come in and warm up, and I'll drive the sleigh for our ride."

"Yes," Sarah said, nodding. "You two go have a romantic little sleigh ride, just the two of you."

Lila felt her cheeks flush at the idea. "I'd love that," she said to Brady.

Outside, Brady helped Lila climb aboard the bench where Tom had been sitting and tucked the heavy blankets around their legs. They sat with their shoulders touching as Brady guided the horse out onto Main Street.

"This is incredible," Lila whispered as they glided down the deserted Main Street. The only sounds were the soft jingle of harness bells and the whisper of sleigh runners over snow. Above them, stars glittered in the clear winter sky, and the quarter moon cast everything in silver light. All the festival lights were still twinkling from the lampposts and storefronts, creating a magical canopy of warm golden light that reflected off the snow.

"One of my favorite parts of Christmas here," Brady said, his voice low in the peaceful atmosphere. "I've been on this ride dozens of times, but it never gets old."

They passed Emily's Yarn & Quilts, its windows glowing softly, then the bakery where they'd bought hot chocolate during the festival. The Christmas tree in the town square stood tall and magnificent, beckoning them toward it.

"It's perfect," Lila breathed, leaning against Brady's warmth as they took in the magical scene. "It's like having the whole town to ourselves."

Brady brought the sleigh to a gentle stop in front of the Christmas tree so they could fully appreciate the scene. "Perfect company too," he said quietly, and when she looked up at him, his green eyes were serious in the moonlight.

The quiet intimacy of the moment made everything feel suspended in time. As she turned back to admire the tree, Brady's gloved hand found hers under the blanket, wrapping around it in a way that felt safe and reassuring.

"Lila," he said softly, and something in his voice made her look up at him. The Christmas tree lights cast a warm glow over his face, highlighting the tenderness in his expression.

Before she could say anything, he leaned down and kissed her. It was gentle and sweet, their cold lips warming against each other. When they broke apart, she could see her breath mingling with his in the cold air.

"I've been wanting to do that again since the tree lighting ceremony," he admitted, his forehead resting against hers.

"Me too," she whispered back, feeling her heart flutter in a way she hadn't experienced in years. She snuggled into his side, resting her head on his strong shoulder.

"So, tell me about your work," Brady said after a moment. "All this traveling you do for consulting. What's your schedule like?"

"It varies," Lila said, grateful to have something other than her adoption to discuss. "Sometimes I'm gone for a week, sometimes just a couple of days. I try not to be away from home more than two weeks at a time, but that doesn't always work out."

"And home is California?"

She nodded. "Huntington Beach. Though honestly, it's never really felt like home. It's just a good base because most of my work is on the West Coast or in Hawaii." She paused. "What about you? Do you ever get time off from the inn?"

Brady was quiet for a moment. "Not much, and probably even less going forward with Tom and Carol slowing down. They've put their whole lives into this place, and they need to know it'll be in good hands."

"That's a big responsibility."

"It is. But it's also what I want. I can't imagine working anywhere but the inn."

There was something wistful in his voice that made her chest tighten. "Would you ever be able to get away? Even for a few days?"

"Maybe in the spring, after the busy season winds down. May is pretty quiet here. We call it 'Mud Season' because the snow has melted too much for winter activities like skiing, but there are still patches making it too muddy for many of the summer activities. A lot of stores and restaurants, here and in Breckenridge, close for the month for repairs or renovations or just a vacation."

She involuntarily shivered from the cold, and Brady wrapped his arm around her. "We should start back before you turn into an icicle." He got the horses going again and they began the gentle ride back toward the inn. "What about you? When's your next project?"

"I don't have anything scheduled until the second week of January. A resort in Scottsdale." The dates suddenly felt significant in a way they hadn't before. "I usually book pretty far out, but I could probably keep my calendar lighter for a while if I wanted to."

"Would you want to?" The question was asked carefully, but she could hear the hope underneath it.

Lila looked at his profile in the moonlight—the strong jaw, the way his wavy brown hair escaped from his wool hat, the gentle way he handled the reins. "I think I might," she said with a smile.

When they reached the inn, the warm glow from the windows seemed even more welcoming than before. After Brady helped her down from the sleigh, he held on tight to her hand and turned her to face him.

"Whatever happens tomorrow with Carol," he said, "I want you to know that this is the most fun I've had in a long time."

"For me too," she admitted. "I came here looking for my birth mother, but I found something I didn't expect to find."

"What's that?"

"People who make me want to slow down." The admission surprised her with its honesty.

Brady leaned down and kissed her again in the soft glow of the inn's lights. It was tender and warmed her from within as he pulled her against him. Winter weather was definitely more tolerable if you had someone like this to help heat things up. At the risk of getting frostbite, she wanted to stay right there in that moment forever. No work deadlines, no grief, no birth mother to find.

When he finally pulled away and they walked together to put away the horses for the night, Lila felt a mixture of anticipation and hope. Tomorrow, she would finally ask Carol the question that had brought her to Pine Ridge. But tonight, for the first time since arriving, she wasn't focused solely on the past. She was beginning to imagine a different kind of future.

Thirteen

When Lila and Brady returned from the barn, the inn was quieter than she'd expected. The lobby glowed softly from the dying embers in the fireplace, but there was no sign of the other guests.

"Where is everyone?" Lila asked, unwinding her scarf.

"I guess everyone turned in already," Brady said, hanging up his coat. "After all, Santa can't come until we're all in bed." He winked at her.

Carol appeared from the kitchen, wiping her hands on a dish towel. She'd changed from her dinner dress into comfortable jeans and a forest green sweater, her hair pulled back.

"How was the sleigh ride?" she asked, but Lila noticed how her eyes didn't quite meet hers directly.

"Magical," Lila said. "The whole town looked like a Christmas card."

"I'm glad." Carol's smile was warm but brief. "I was just setting up the breakfast casseroles to go in the oven first thing in the morning. Christmas breakfast is always a production."

Brady glanced between Lila and Carol, seeming to sense the undercurrent of tension. "I should go check on the horses, make sure they're settled for the night." He caught Lila's eye. "Take your time."

The pointed comment wasn't lost on either woman. Brady was giving them space to speak alone. Lila's stomach fluttered with nerves. She hadn't planned to have this conversation tonight. She'd planned to lie awake most of the night rehearsing what she wanted to say tomorrow, but this seemed like as good a time as any.

"Can I help with anything?" Lila offered as Brady disappeared out the back door.

"That's sweet of you, but I'm nearly finished." Carol moved toward the kitchen, and Lila followed. "Just need to get these covered and refrigerated now that they've had time to cool."

The kitchen was warm and cozy, fragrant with the scent of bacon and cheese from the casseroles. Carol moved efficiently between the counter and refrigerator, covering glass baking dishes with foil and making space on the shelves. Lila watched her hands—the same long fingers she'd noticed before that looked like her own.

"Carol," Lila began, then stopped. Her heart was hammering against her ribs.

"Yes, dear?" Carol's voice was gentle, but she kept her attention focused on the casseroles.

Lila took a breath. There was no graceful way to ease into this. "I need to ask you something."

Carol's hands stilled on the foil she was smoothing over a dish. "All right."

"When I mentioned at dinner that I was looking for information about my birth mother, you seemed . . ." Lila paused, struggling for the right words. "You seemed upset."

"Did I?" Carol's voice was carefully neutral, but she still wasn't looking at Lila directly.

"You left the table so quickly." Lila moved closer, her voice growing softer. "Carol, I found out that the quilt my birth mother sent with me was delivered here. To Pine Ridge Inn on Christmas Eve, 1991."

Carol's shoulders tensed, and she turned slowly to face Lila. Her eyes were bright with unshed tears.

"The night before I was born," Lila continued, her voice barely above a whisper. "Carol, I have to ask—are you my mother?"

For a long moment, the only sound was the hum of the refrigerator. Carol's face crumpled with emotion, and she pressed a hand to her chest.

"Oh, Lila." Carol's voice was thick with tears. "Sweetheart, no. I'm not your birth mother."

The words hit Lila like a physical blow. She'd been so certain, had built up the possibility in her mind until it felt like reality. "You're not?"

"No, honey." Carol reached for her hands, gripping them tightly. "But I would have been so lucky, so incredibly blessed, to have a daughter like you."

Lila felt tears spill over, disappointment and confusion mixing together. "But the way you reacted, and the baby ornament, and—"

"I know." Carol's own tears were falling freely now. "I know how it must have looked. But Lila, the reason I got emotional wasn't because you're my daughter. It's because—" She stopped, seeming to wrestle with something.

"Because what?"

Carol was quiet for a long moment, her thumb rubbing gently over Lila's knuckles. "Because I do know who your mother is, dear."

Lila's breath caught. "What?"

"I know you want answers, but Lila, it's not my story to tell."

"Please." Lila gripped Carol's hands tighter. "I've come so far to find answers. I can't get this close and not find out."

"The person involved deserves to make her own choice about whether to share her story with you." Carol's expression was gentle but firm as she gave Lila's hands a final squeeze before letting them go. "She knows you're here now, and I have to leave it up to her whether she wants to come forward."

"You've spoken with her?" Lila asked, her voice frantic. "You know how to get in touch with her?"

Carol nodded. "I have. Please be patient and give her time to digest the news. You've had some time to think on it, but this was very unexpected for her."

Lila's mind was racing. What had Carol told this woman about Lila? Sure, Carol liked her, and they seemed to have a connection, but had she talked Lila up? Told the woman she had enjoyed her time with her so much that she wished Lila was her own daughter?

"I was so certain it was you," Lila said, leaning back against the counter for support as her legs began to feel shaky underneath her.

Carol wiped at the tears remaining on her face. "You were right that the baby ornament and some of the things I've said pointed to me having given up a child. But the truth is, Tom and I lost a baby. Early in our marriage, I miscarried at about four months along."

Lila's chest tightened with sympathy. "Carol, I'm so sorry."

"It was devastating at the time. We'd been trying for so long, and then when we finally got pregnant . . ." Fresh tears threatened to spill from her eyes. "We never got pregnant again after that. So when I see baby things, when I talk about the children we might have had, I'm thinking about the baby we lost, not one I gave away."

The explanation made perfect sense, and Lila felt foolish for not considering it. Of course, Carol's emotional reactions could stem from loss rather than a secret she'd kept hidden.

"That's why your story tonight hit me so hard," Carol continued. "Here you are, this wonderful young woman looking for her birth mother, and it just made me think about what might have been. What our baby might have grown up to be like. It took me a few minutes before I put the pieces together and realized who you really are."

Lila wanted to push for more about her birth mother, but something in the older woman's expression warned her not to press further tonight.

"I understand," Lila said finally. "And I'm sorry for assuming—"

"Don't apologize, sweetheart. Your instincts weren't completely wrong. I would love nothing more than to claim you as my daughter." Carol gave her a loving smile.

As Lila reached out to hug her, she couldn't help wishing Carol was her mother. Not just so the mystery would be solved but because she'd genuinely grown to love her.

"Get some sleep, sweetheart. Tomorrow is Christmas and your birthday. Let's make it a day worth celebrating." Carol squeezed her shoulder. "Whatever happens, you've found a family here who loves you. I hope you know that."

As Lila made her way upstairs, disappointment weighed heavy in her chest. She'd been so certain Carol was her birth mother, had built up the possibility until it felt real. Now, not only was she back to square one, but it was largely out of her control. She would have to wait for her mother to come to her.

In her room, Lila sat on the edge of the bed and stared out at the snow-covered town. Somewhere out there was the woman who'd given her life, and now she knew Lila was looking for her. But in a way, Lila felt no closer to finding her than she had when she'd first arrived in Pine Ridge.

Fourteen

Lila had barely slept. Every time she'd drifted off, she'd jolted awake thinking about Carol's words: "I do know who your mother is." Someone knew she was here and was deciding what might happen next. Knowing someone was out there debating whether they wanted to meet her was worse than having no leads at all.

She'd spent most of the night staring at the ceiling, wondering who her birth mother could be. Had she been too young to raise a baby on her own? Had she never wanted children and gotten pregnant by accident? Had she ever regretted her decision?

Around five-thirty, pale light filtered through her curtains. Lila pulled them back to find fresh snow falling on the already white landscape, the world hushed and pristine in the pre-dawn quiet. Movement in the yard below caught her eye.

Brady was outside, methodically shoveling the walkway from the inn to Main Street. Even in the dim morning light, she could see the rhythm of his work. Watching him made something in her chest ease slightly. At least she had someone she could confide in about everything. Sure, she could call Jenna, but she was no doubt having a busy Christmas morning with her own family. It was Brady who knew Carol and how badly Lila had begun to hope she was her birth mother.

Lila pulled on warm clothes and made her way downstairs. The lobby was quiet except for the soft ticking of the grandfather clock in the corner. She grabbed her coat from the hook by the door and stepped out into the crisp morning air. Her breath formed small clouds that reminded her of a locomotive as she made her way down the newly shoveled path.

"Merry Christmas," Brady called when he saw her approaching. Snow clung to his dark hair and the shoulders of his coat. "And happy birthday."

"Thank you. Merry Christmas to you too," she said, although without the same enthusiasm with which he'd delivered the greeting.

When she reached him, he leaned down and kissed her on the cheek. "You're up early."

"Couldn't sleep," she admitted.

"Tell me about it while we feed the horses?"

"Sure. I could use the distraction."

She followed him silently around the corner of the inn toward the stables.

The barn was warm and fragrant with the scent of hay and horses. Thunder nickered softly when he saw them, and Buttercup tossed her golden mane in greeting. There was something soothing about the simple routine of filling water troughs and measuring out grain. And running her hand down Thunder's nose had a calming effect.

"So," Brady said after they'd worked in companionable silence for several minutes, "how did your conversation with Carol go last night?"

Lila leaned against Thunder's stall, watching the horse eat. "She's not my birth mother."

Brady paused in his work with the feed buckets. "I'm sorry. I know how certain you were."

"The worst part is that she knows who is." Lila's voice came out smaller than she'd intended. "She said she's contacted my birth mother and that it's up to her whether she wants to reveal herself."

Brady set down the bucket and moved closer, his expression concerned. "So, your birth mother knows you're here?"

"Apparently. Carol said I needed to give her time to process the news." Lila wrapped her arms around herself, suddenly feeling vulnerable. "What if she decides she doesn't want to meet me? What if seeing me would just bring up painful memories she'd rather keep buried?"

"Or what if she's been hoping for this moment for thirty-four years?" Brady's voice was gentle but firm. "Lila, you can't know her reasons for the original adoption or how she's felt about it all these years. Maybe she's been waiting for you to find her."

"Carol said essentially the same thing last night." Lila managed a small smile. "She also said she would have been lucky to have me as a daughter, which was incredibly sweet but also made me realize how much I'd started picturing it was her."

Brady reached over and tucked a strand of hair behind her ear, his touch gentle. "Carol's not wrong. Anyone would be lucky to have you in their life."

The simple statement, delivered with quiet conviction, made tears prick her eyes. "I don't know what to do now. Just wait and hope she decides she wants to meet me?"

"I think that's all you can do. But Lila, remember that no matter what happens, you've found people who care about you here." Brady's green eyes were serious in the soft barn lighting. "That's not nothing."

"I know. And I'm grateful for all of it, especially for you." She looked up at him, this man who'd become so much more than she'd expected when she first arrived in Pine Ridge. "I just feel like I'm so close to answers, but that they're completely out of my control."

"The important things in life usually are out of our control," Brady said softly. "But I find they're often worth waiting for."

They finished with the horses and made their way back toward the inn, where warm light was beginning to glow from the kitchen windows. The rest of the world was still quiet, but Lila could see Carol moving around inside, preparing for the day's festivities.

"Whatever happens today," Brady said as they reached the porch steps, "I'm glad you decided to stay."

He leaned down, pressing a kiss to her lips. It was gentle and sweet, and as soon as he pulled away, she missed the warmth of his lips on hers.

"I'm glad I decided to stay too," Lila said, and meant it. Whatever uncertainty lay ahead about her birth mother, she was increasingly certain she was catching feelings for Brady. And like he had said, that wasn't nothing.

By the time they'd returned from the barn and cleaned up, the inn was coming alive with Christmas morning energy. The scent of cinnamon rolls and coffee drifted from the kitchen, and Lila could hear voices and laughter from the dining room.

"Merry Christmas, you two!" Kimberly called out when they appeared in the lobby. She was already dressed in a festive red sweater, her hair pulled back with a sparkly headband. "Brady, Carol's been looking for you. Something about the coffee machine."

"Maybe someone should have asked Santa for a Brew Pro 11 after all," Lila teased.

"Nah, I was saving my Christmas wish for something even better," he winked at her before turning to head to the kitchen.

In the dining room, another feast awaited the group. The table was set with china that had tiny holly leaves with red berries around the edges of the plates, and the breakfast spread looked like something from a magazine. Fresh fruit was arranged in the shape of a Christmas tree, and thick-cut bacon lay mounded next to the tray of cinnamon rolls. The breakfast casseroles Carol had prepped the night before completed the buffet.

"This is incredible, Carol," Ali said, already filling her plate. "I can't believe you got up early enough to prepare all this."

"Sarah helped me prep the casseroles last night and make the fruit tree, and the rest was easy," Carol replied.

Brady appeared with a fresh pot of coffee, refilling every-one's mugs. "Speaking of Sarah, has anyone seen her yet this morning or is she sleeping in?" he asked as he reached Lila's place at the table.

Lila had completely forgotten about their usual morn-ing coffee date in her haste to go tell Brady about the conversation with Carol. It was becoming a treasured part of her day, and she hated that she'd missed it.

"She's not feeling well," Carol said, glancing toward the stairs with concern. "She sent word down that she's going to rest in her room today. I offered to bring her some breakfast, but she said she just needs to sleep."

Lila felt a pang of disappointment. Sarah had been such a steady, comforting presence all week, and she loved Christmas. Lila hated that she wasn't feeling well and couldn't enjoy the day's festivities. Maybe she'd be able to join the group later that afternoon after she'd rested up some.

As they finished up breakfast, Sophie began tapping her fork against her juice glass. "Before we disperse," she announced, "Miles and I have a little surprise for everyone if you can join us in the lobby."

They all followed Sophie and Miles and sat down on the couch and chairs closest to the Christmas tree they'd all helped decorate only a few days before. Lila noticed there were now presents under the tree that hadn't been there the night before, and Miles picked up two of them. "We picked up a few little things at the festival for everyone," he explained. "Nothing fancy, just a small token of appre-ciation for such a wonderful week."

"You didn't have to do that," Carol protested, but her eyes were bright with pleasure.

"Nonsense," Sophie said, helping Miles distribute packages. "Christmas is about sharing, and you've all made this such a special holiday for us."

The gift exchange that followed was warm and heartfelt. Sophie and Miles had chosen thoughtfully—a hand-carved ornament for Carol and Tom that featured the outline of buildings on Main Street, locally-made soaps for the sisters, a beautiful bookmark made from pressed mountain flowers for Ali, an etched highball glass for Mike with Breckenridge's ski slopes, and a handmade leather wallet for Brady. They'd given Lila a small pottery coffee mug with "Pine Ridge" painted on it in delicate script.

"So you'll remember us when you're back home and having your morning coffee," Sophie said with a wink.

"As if I could forget," Lila said, touched by the gesture.

Some of the other guests ran upstairs to bring down more small gifts, and soon the lobby was scattered with wrapping paper, and everyone was admiring their presents. Ali had found small bottles of locally-made maple syrup for everyone, and the sisters had bought everyone pine-scented candles. Lila felt bad that she had been so preoccupied with her own reasons for being in town that she hadn't thought of anyone else, but thankfully Mike and Ali had been too busy skiing to do so either. She would get everyone's addresses and send them something fun from California as a surprise.

As breakfast wound down and people began to disperse, Carol appeared at Lila's elbow.

"Have you heard—" Lila began, then stopped herself. Of course, Carol would have told her if she had any news.

Carol seemed to understand. "Nothing yet, sweetheart. But the day is still young." She reached over and squeezed Lila's hand. "Try to enjoy Christmas morning. Whatever happens will happen when it's meant to."

The rest of Christmas morning passed in a blur of activity. The group gathered around the tree to admire their ornaments in daylight, Tom told stories around the fire about Christmases past at the inn, the group gathered around the dining room table to play board games, and Ali received regular updates from her sister, whose labor was progressing slowly but steadily.

"Still no baby," Ali announced as she and Mike brought the last of their luggage downstairs, "but the doctor says everything looks good. She might be a Christmas Day baby after all."

"How exciting," Carol said. "Christmas babies are special." She turned her warm eyes on Lila when she said this.

Lila wondered how her birth mother felt every year on the holiday. Did she think of Lila? Imagine who she'd become? Lila had certainly thought of her birth mother every year on Christmas, but this was the first one where she'd felt such an intense need to connect with her.

Mike and Ali hugged everyone goodbye, promising to stay in touch. With time for one more game, the rest of the group gathered around the fireplace with an easel that held a giant pad of paper. After a hilarious round of Pictionary, Carol told everyone they had time to freshen up before dinner and asked them to be back down at 5:30.

Lila decided to stop and check on Sarah on her way to her room, knocking lightly on the door in case she was asleep. Sarah didn't answer, so Lila quietly tiptoed down the hall to her room to brush her hair and change into something nicer for dinner.

When Lila descended the stairs at 5:25, she was surprised to find the lobby eerily quiet. Was everyone still in their rooms?

She heard a noise coming from the dining room and went to see who was there. She walked in to find a beautifully decorated cake blazing with candles and everyone standing at the far end of the table.

"Happy Birthday!" everyone shouted in unison before launching into the traditional birthday song.

Lila felt tears spring to her eyes as she looked around at these people who'd become so important to her in just a matter of days. Sophie and Miles were singing with gusto, the sisters had found party hats somewhere and were wearing them with glee, Brady was grinning at her from across the room, and even Tom joined in with his deep bass voice.

"Make a wish," Carol said as she set the cake down in front of Lila.

Lila didn't hesitate. She made the only wish that mattered: Let me find the answers I came here looking for. When she opened her eyes and blew out the candles, everyone cheered.

"What did you wish for?" Kimberly asked as Carol began cutting the cake.

"If I tell you, it won't come true," Lila said with a smile. "Cake before dinner?" she asked Carol.

"You know how it is," she said, smiling like she was letting Lila in on a secret. "If I let everyone eat dinner first, they'll be too full for cake. Since it's a special occasion, I say we start with cake and worry about dinner later. We're only having leftovers tonight anyway. Last night was the big feast."

As they indulged, everyone shared stories about memorable birthdays. Lila felt overwhelmed by the thoughtfulness of these people who'd planned this celebration for her. It was exactly what she'd needed, even if she hadn't known it.

Later, after they'd heated up leftovers and shared more holiday stories, they reflected on their time together. Everyone would be departing tomorrow.

"This has been the most wonderful Christmas," Sophie said as the celebration began to wind down. "Thank you all for making us feel so welcome."

"It's been our pleasure," Carol said, but her eyes kept drifting toward the stairs.

As the group began to disperse, some heading to their rooms to rest and others settling by the fire with books or games, Lila found herself both grateful for the birthday celebration and anxious about what the rest of Christmas might bring. Might she still get her birthday wish?

Brady appeared at her side as she helped clear plates. "Good birthday so far?" he asked quietly.

"The best," she said, and meant it.

Carol returned from taking things back to the kitchen and asked Brady to go outside and get some more logs for the fire.

Once they were alone in the dining room, Carol said quietly, "Before you go, I wanted to share something with you about the night you were born. I know you want more than I can give you right now, but I feel like I can give you this much."

Lila's breath caught. "You remember that night?"

"How could I forget?" She laughed. "It's not every night a baby is born at the inn. The snow was coming down something fierce, and we had a guest who went into labor unexpectedly on Christmas Eve." Carol's voice grew soft with memory. "I was still fairly new to working here, but it was all-hands-on-deck while the paramedics tried to get to us through the storm. I'll never forget how brave that young woman was, laboring through the night while the storm raged outside."

"Was she alone?" Lila asked, her voice barely above a whisper.

"She was visiting alone, yes, but she had all of us around her. And when you were born, just as Christmas Day began, there was so much love in that room, Lila. So much love and such difficult decisions being made out of that love."

Tears sprang to Lila's eyes. "Thank you for telling me that. I can't believe you were there that night."

Carol smiled warmly. "It was an honor to witness your arrival into this world, sweetheart. You were loved and cared for from your very first breath, even if the circumstances were complicated. No matter what, I want you to know that."

As Carol squeezed her hand and headed toward the kitchen, Lila felt something settle in her chest. Whatever happened next, she knew that she'd entered the world surrounded by love, not abandonment. That knowledge felt like a gift in itself.

Fifteen

Lila climbed the stairs slowly, still glowing from the surprise birthday celebration. It had been everything she'd needed for her first Christmas without either of her parents. She'd laughed and smiled all day, able to push aside the doubts and fears about her birth mother and whether she'd ever meet her.

"Lila?" Sarah's voice was soft behind her.

Lila turned to find Sarah standing outside her own room. She really did look sick, her face pale and drawn.

"I heard you weren't feeling well," Lila said, moving closer with concern. "Are you okay? Can I get you anything?"

"No dear," Sarah said, her voice barely above a whisper. "I'm okay." She took a shaky breath. "Could we talk? Privately?"

"Of course. Would you like to come into my room?"

Sarah nodded, following Lila down the hall. Inside the Pinecone Room, Lila flipped on the bedside lamp, then turned to offer Sarah the wingback chair by the window.

But Sarah wasn't looking at the chair. Her gaze was fixed on the bed, where Lila's baby quilt lay folded at the foot. If it were even possible, Sarah's face went even whiter than it had been in the hall.

"Sarah?" Lila moved toward her, alarmed. "What is it? Are you okay?"

Sarah approached the bed with trembling steps, her hand reaching out to touch the quilt as if it might dissolve into smoke at the contact. Her fingers traced the red, green, and white squares with reverent care.

"It's exactly like I remember," Sarah whispered, her voice thick with emotion.

Lila's breath caught in her throat. "What did you just say?"

Sarah's fingers continued their gentle exploration of the fabric, tears beginning to stream down her cheeks. "I chose this quilt for my baby girl."

The words hit Lila like a physical blow. The room seemed to tilt around her as she stared at Sarah, this woman who'd been so kind to her all week, who'd understood her grief about losing her mother, who'd felt like such a comforting presence.

Lila's voice came out as barely a whisper. "You're my birth mother?"

Sarah lifted her tear-filled eyes to meet Lila's. "Yes, sweetheart. I am."

Lila sank onto the edge of the bed, her legs suddenly unable to support her. "I can't believe this. You've been right here the entire time."

"I didn't know it until what you said at dinner last night. I was so surprised that I needed time to think about what I could say to you. How I could explain what I did."

Sarah sat in the wingback chair, pulling a tissue from her pocket to dab at her eyes. "I've been coming back to Pine Ridge every Christmas for thirty-four years. At first, I told myself it was because this was the last place I'd been truly happy with David. But really, I think I've been coming back because it's where you were born. It's the closest I could get to you."

"David," Lila repeated, remembering Sarah's story from their walk in the woods. "Your husband who died."

"Your father," Sarah corrected gently. "He died from a very aggressive cancer before you were born. We hadn't even been married two years yet."

Lila felt tears burning her eyes as pieces of the puzzle began falling into place. "You came back here because you'd spent Christmas here with him the year before."

She nodded. "Our first Christmas as husband and wife. We were so happy, so full of plans for the future." Sarah's voice broke. "When he died, I felt like my world ended. I was twenty-three years old, pregnant, and completely alone. I didn't know how I could possibly raise a child on my own—emotionally or financially. I couldn't even take care of myself in those months after he died."

"So you came back here to have me?" Lila said, trying to process everything she was hearing.

"You weren't due for another month. I came back because I couldn't bear to be anywhere else on Christmas. This inn, this town—it held so many happy memories from our only Christmas together as husband and wife." Sarah wiped at her tears with the back of her hand. "I went into labor early on Christmas Eve. The storm was so bad the paramedics almost couldn't get through. Carol and

Tom were there, and Tom's parents, and they all took such good care of us."

"Carol told me tonight she remembered there was so much love in the room when I was born." Tears were streaking down Lila's face now.

Sarah nodded. "There was. Even in the middle of my grief and fear, there was so much love for you. But I was drowning, Lila. The pain of losing David was so fresh, and I was terrified I wouldn't be enough for you. I wanted you to have everything—two parents, stability, a real chance at happiness. I'd quit my job and was living off what little savings we had, and I couldn't afford to keep our house without David's salary. I could barely even get out of bed most mornings. Then I resolved to come here, and it felt like kismet that you decided to be born here where David and I had spent such a magical week."

Lila studied Sarah's face, seeing her own features reflected there for the first time. The same brown eyes, the same heart shape to their face, even similar gestures she'd noticed but hadn't understood.

"I worked with the adoption agency for months, looking at profiles of potential parents. I was so particular about choosing the right family for you." Sarah's voice grew stronger, more certain. "When I saw your parents' profile, I knew immediately they were perfect. They were older, established, desperate for a child to love. I could see in their photos how much joy they would bring to your life."

"They did," Lila said softly. "They gave me everything I could have ever wanted."

"I'm so grateful for that," Sarah whispered. "All these years, I've prayed that whoever raised you was giving you the love and opportunities you deserved."

"Why did you seal the records?" Lila could finally ask the question that had bothered her for years. "If you loved me, why make it so I couldn't ever find you?"

Sarah's face crumpled with fresh tears. "The agency counselor said it would be better for everyone. She said it would be a clean break so I could move on, and you could bond completely with your new family. It seemed logical at the time, but I regretted it almost immediately. By then, it was too late to change it. Five years ago, I did one of those DNA tests. I kept hoping you'd do one and we'd find each other that way. I never imagined we'd meet like this, without knowing who each other were."

They sat in silence for a moment, both overwhelmed by the magnitude of what had just been revealed. Lila looked at this woman who'd been such a comfort to her all week, who'd understood her grief and loneliness in ways that made perfect sense.

"So, you thought about me sometimes?"

"Oh, honey," Sarah came to sit by Lila on the bed, taking Lila's hand in her own. "Of course I did. Every single day for the last thirty-four years. I hoped and prayed you were having a beautiful life, and I tried to find ways to atone for what I did. I became a school counselor because I wanted to help children who were struggling, who felt alone or unwanted. I kept thinking that somewhere out there, my daughter might need someone like that in her life, and maybe if I helped other children, someone would be helping you too."

The selflessness of it made Lila's chest tight with emotion. "All these years, you've been trying to take care of me indirectly."

"It was the only way I knew how. I never stopped thinking about you. Wondering who you'd become, what you looked like, if you were happy." Sarah's voice was barely a whisper. "When you told us why you were here last night, I could barely breathe. My baby, my daughter, was right here with me. And I already loved you from the time we'd spent together, and I was so afraid you wouldn't feel the same when I told you the truth."

"Is that why you hid in your room today? You weren't sick?"

"I was terrified," Sarah admitted. "I was afraid that when you found out the truth, you'd hate me for giving you up. For not fighting harder to keep you. For making a choice that changed both our lives forever."

Lila looked at Sarah's tear-streaked face, at the fear and love in her brown eyes. She thought about the woman who'd raised her, who'd always told her that her birth mother must have loved her very much to make such a difficult choice. She thought about Sarah's career spent caring for other people's children, about her annual pilgrimages to Pine Ridge, about the grief and loneliness that had shaped thirty-four years of both of their lives.

"I don't hate you," Lila said finally. "I could never hate you. What you did—giving me up so I could have a better life—that was love. The purest kind of love."

Sarah's sob was audible as she reached for Lila, pulling her into an embrace that felt like coming home. They held each other as thirty-four years of separation melted away, both crying for the lost time and the love that had never really been lost at all.

"I've missed you so much," Sarah whispered against her hair. "Every Christmas, every birthday, every milestone you had that I wasn't there for."

Sarah cupped Lila's face in her hands, studying her features with wonder. "You're so beautiful, so accomplished, so kind. Your parents did such a wonderful job raising you."

"They did," Lila agreed. "But they would have understood this. They always told me that if I ever wanted to find you, they would support me completely."

"They sound like amazing people."

"They were. You absolutely chose the perfect parents for me. And now I know where I get some of my traits from too." Lila managed a watery smile. "I think maybe I have your eyes."

Sarah nodded. "Passed down from my mother." She reached up and stroked Lila's hair like she was seeing it for the first time.

They sat together on the bed, holding hands and looking at the quilt that had brought them together after decades of separation. Outside the window, snow was falling on Pine Ridge, the town where their story had begun and where it was finally, beautifully, continuing.

"What happens now?" Lila asked, her voice small and uncertain despite the joy flooding her heart.

"Now we get to know each other," Sarah said, squeezing her hands. "We have thirty-four years to catch up on, and if you're willing, we could even build a future together."

"I'd like that," Lila whispered. "I'd like that very much."

The Christmas miracle Lila had been hoping for had been sitting right beside her all along.

Sixteen

Lila and Sarah promised to talk more in the morning as
Sarah retired to her room to rest. Brady was expecting
Lila downstairs to watch a movie with the group, and
she had to tell someone what had just happened. She'd
asked Sarah's permission to share it with Brady, which she
assured Lila she understood.

"You know, I've watched that young man grow up from
one Christmas to the next. He's a good one. You can trust
him with your heart," Sarah said, hugging Lila one last
time in the hallway.

By the time Lila made her way downstairs, the group
had gathered in the lobby around the television. Tom was
adjusting the volume while Carol distributed mugs of hot
cocoa topped with whipped cream and cinnamon.

"Perfect timing," Carol said when she saw them. "We're
just starting *It's a Wonderful Life*. It's become a bit of a
Christmas tradition here."

Lila caught Brady's eye across the room, and he immediately seemed to sense that something had changed. He
got up and came over to meet her.

"Everything okay?"

She nodded. "Could we go somewhere to talk?"

Carol glanced between them with knowing eyes. "Take your time, you two. We'll probably watch another movie after this one if you want to join us later."

Outside, fresh snow crunched under their boots as they made their way along a path that led to a small log cabin tucked among the pine trees behind the main inn. It was rustic but well-maintained, with a covered porch and warm light glowing from the windows.

"Welcome to my humble abode," Brady said, opening the front door.

The interior was cozy and masculine, with exposed wooden beams and a stone fireplace. But what immediately caught Lila's attention were the paintings that covered nearly every wall. There were landscapes in watercolor and oil that featured snow-covered mountains or endless fields of mountain wildflowers.

"Are these all your mother's?" Lila asked, moving closer to study a particularly stunning painting of the inn during autumn, surrounded by golden aspens.

"Every one." Brady moved to the fireplace and began building a fire. "I couldn't bear to put them in storage. This way, it's like she's still here with me."

Among all the landscapes, one portrait stood out. It appeared to be a young Brady, perhaps six or seven years old, grinning gap-toothed at the viewer. His mother had captured a lifelike quality about him in those brushstrokes. Lila recognized the kindness in his eyes and the hint of mischief in his smile.

"She was incredibly talented," Lila said. "And she clearly adored you."

"The feeling was mutual." Brady glanced up from the kindling he was arranging. "When I close my eyes, I can still see her in her studio painting these."

The fire caught, casting a warm glow throughout the small living room. Brady settled onto the couch, patting the space beside him. Lila joined him, still feeling like she was floating outside her body.

"So," Brady said gently, "what's on your mind? It seemed important."

Lila took a shaky breath. "Brady, I found her. I found my birth mother."

His eyes widened. "Carol told you who it was?"

"She didn't have to." Lila turned to face him fully. "Brady, it's Sarah."

The words hung in the air between them. Brady stared at her, processing what she'd said.

"Sarah," he repeated slowly. "Like our Sarah here at the inn?"

"She found me in the hall when I went upstairs after dinner. She's been coming back to Pine Ridge every Christmas for thirty-four years because this is where I was born. Her husband—my father—died three months before I was born, and she didn't think she was prepared to raise a child alone."

Brady reached for her hand. "Wow, that's incredible. I've spent every Christmas with her for nearly twenty years, and I've never heard her say anything about having a baby. How are you processing all of this?"

"I don't know." She laughed, a sound caught between joy and disbelief. "Part of me can't believe it. I mean, what are the odds? But another part of me feels like it makes perfect sense. I felt a connection with her from the very first day, and she understood my grief at such a deep level. I always felt better when I was around her."

"She adores you," Brady said simply. "Anyone could see that from the way she looks at you, even before you both knew the truth."

Lila told him everything—the surprise Christmas Eve birth, regretting her decision to close the adoption, doing the DNA test hoping to find Lila, and not knowing until Lila mentioned the quilt and her reason for visiting the night before.

"She spent her entire career working with children because she thought maybe someone would help me the same way she was helping other kids." Tears spilled over again. "She's been loving me from a distance for thirty-four years."

Brady pulled her into his arms, holding her as she cried against his shoulder. They sat like that for several minutes, the fire crackling softly and the snow falling outside the windows.

"Are you going to tell the others?" Brady asked eventually.

"Not tonight. Sarah was terrified to tell me the truth. She spent all day hiding in her room because she was afraid I'd hate her for giving me up. I think we both need time to process this before we make it public. Obviously, Carol and Tom know, and I did ask her if I could tell you."

Brady nodded. "This is huge for both of you."

Lila pulled back to look at him. "There's something else. It's probably a little impulsive, and I haven't really thought it through, but I was looking through resorts with requests for proposals when I couldn't sleep last night, and I saw one over in Breckenridge. Initially, I was thinking it might let me be closer to you . . ." She paused, waiting for his reaction.

"That sounds incredible," he said taking her hand in his again. "Poor guys won't know what's hit them."

She smirked at him. "Funny. You know, some people actually *want* me to make changes to their hotels. Anyway—I haven't had any time to think about this yet—but it would put me closer to Sarah too so we could spend more time getting to know each other."

"I know she lives here in Colorado somewhere. Colorado Springs?"

Lila shook her head. "No, just outside of Denver. She works at an elementary school there."

Brady's expression grew hopeful. "How long would a project like that take?"

"Three to six months, depending on the scope." She looked at him carefully. "I'm thinking about applying for it."

"You'd move here? For six months?"

"I'd move here to be close to Sarah, to figure out what kind of relationship we can build. And I'd move here to be close to you." She felt heat rise in her cheeks. "You know, if you wanted more of me and my obnoxious suggestions."

"Lila, if you'll come back, I'll listen to all your suggestions. Maybe I'll even try one, just for fun." Brady's smile was so bright it could have powered the cabin. "But what about your condo? Your friends? Are you normally gone this long for a project?"

"I can sublet the condo, and I never really put down roots in Huntington Beach." Lila shifted closer to him on the couch. "The truth is, I came here looking for my past, and I think maybe I found my future instead."

Brady cupped her face in his hands. "I have to warn you, if you hang around here more, I might just fall for you.

"I might just fall for you too," she whispered back.

He kissed her then, soft and sweet and full of promise. When they broke apart, he rested his forehead against hers.

"So, you'll really stay? For six months?"

"If I get the consulting job, yes. And after that . . ." She shrugged. "We'll figure it out as we go."

They sat in comfortable silence, watching the fire and processing everything that had changed in the span of a few hours. Through the window, Lila could see the lights of the inn twinkling through the snow-covered trees.

Snow was continuing to fall on Pine Ridge, blanketing the town where Lila had been born, where she'd found her birth mother, and where she was beginning to believe her future might unfold. Tomorrow, other guests would begin departing, and she and Sarah would have to decide what came next. But tonight, in Brady's arms, Lila felt perfectly, completely at peace.

She'd come to Pine Ridge looking for answers about her past. She'd found that, along with people she'd never known she was looking for.

Seventeen

Lila woke to sunlight filtering through the curtains. For a moment, she lay still, remembering everything that had happened the night before. Sarah. Her birth mother had been right here with her all week. She'd been someone Lila had felt instantly connected to, even before she knew the truth.

Lila pulled out her phone so she could share the news with Jenna.

"Please tell me you're calling with good news about the lumberjack," Jenna said as soon as she answered.

"His name is Brady, and yes, but that's not why I'm calling." Lila settled back against her pillows, still in disbelief about what she was about to say. "Jen, I found her."

"You were right? It was Carol?" Jenna asked excitedly.

"No, it wasn't her. I ended up asking her about it, and she said she wished she was but that she'd had a miscarriage and never been able to have children. But . . . she did know who it was and wanted to let them make the decision whether to tell me. And it turned out she's been here the entire time! Her name is Sarah, and she's one of the other guests. We've been having coffee together every morning, talking about all sorts of things. We had this immediate bond."

"Oh my God, Lila." Jenna's voice was breathless. "So, she just came out and admitted it? Had she suspected it all along?"

Lila told her about the quilt, about Sarah's reaction, about the conversation in her room where everything came together, about her birth father, David. She could hear Jenna crying on the other end of the line.

"She's been coming back here every Christmas for thirty-four years because this is where I was born," Lila continued. "She never stopped thinking about me."

"That's incredible. How are you feeling? Are you okay?"

"I'm . . ." Lila searched for the right words. "I'm overwhelmed in the best possible way. She's exactly the kind of person I hoped she'd be. Gentle and caring and she became a school counselor because she wanted to help other children as a way to sort of atone for giving me up."

"That's beautiful," Jenna said softly. "What happens now?"

"We're going to stay here for a few more days, just the two of us. Then I'm going to visit her in Denver and see her life there."

"I'm so happy for you," Jenna said, and Lila could hear the genuine joy in her voice. "You deserve this, Lila. You deserve to have family and love and a place that feels like home."

They talked for a few more minutes, Jenna asking questions about Sarah and then begging for a Brady update, which Lila was happy to give.

"So, you're going to apply for the Breckenridge job so you can spend more time with both of them?"

"Yep. It would be the perfect situation if I can land it."

"Everyone wants highly sought after Lila McAllister to turn their resort around," Jenna said with a full vote of confidence.

They said their goodbyes, and Lila promised to call and update her after she spent a few more days with Sarah.

Her thoughts turning to Sarah, she wondered if Sarah was waiting for her at their usual spot for coffee this morning. Would it be awkward once she'd had another night to sleep on it?

Lila's stomach did a little flip-flop when she saw the top of Sarah's head in her usual chair at the end of the hall in the little nook.

Sarah turned as Lila approached. "Good morning," she said with a warmth that made Lila's chest tighten with emotion.

"Good morning," Lila said, walking over to grab a mug for the machine. Suddenly, she was too nervous to look at Sarah. How were they supposed to act now that they both knew the truth?

"How did you sleep?" Sarah asked.

"Better than I have in months," Lila admitted, pressing the start button and turning away from the machine. "What about you?"

"For the first time in thirty-four years, I didn't spend Christmas night wondering where you were or if you were happy." Sarah's smile was radiant. "I slept like a baby."

"Me too," Lila agreed.

They both watched out the window in comfortable silence for a few minutes as a light snow started to fall outside. Lila had just retrieved her now full cup of coffee from the machine and turned back toward the window when two deer emerged from the tree line. It looked like the same mother and young deer from their first morning together.

"They're back," Lila observed.

"Maybe they were a sign. We just didn't know it yet."

Lila smiled over at Sarah. "I think you're right."

"Lila," Sarah said as if broaching something even more sensitive than the conversation they were already having, "I want to run something by you."

"Yes?"

Sarah turned to face her fully. "I don't want to hide this anymore. I've spent thirty-four years keeping this secret, carrying this sadness alone. But I don't want to hide my joy about finding you. This group has become like family to both of us this week. They've been part of this journey, even without knowing it."

Lila felt her heart swell. "You want to tell them?"

"Only if you're comfortable with it. But Lila, look what happened this week. We were strangers seven days ago, and now we're sitting here as a family. Sophie and Miles, Kimberly and Kendall, even Ali and Mike—they've all been part of creating that magic. I think they deserve to know how the story ends, but only if you're comfortable with that."

Lila nodded. "I'd love to tell them. You're right. They have become family."

"There's something else," Sarah said, her voice growing more tentative. "I know you need to get back to your life in California and your work. But I was hoping . . . would you consider staying in Pine Ridge for a few more days? Just you and me? I asked Carol already, and the inn is empty the next few days until some New Year's Eve guests arrive."

The invitation made Lila's eyes well with tears. "I would love that. I don't need to be back home until after the New Year."

Sarah's face lit up. "Maybe after we spend a few days here, you might want to come back to Denver with me and see a little of my life there?"

"Absolutely. I think that would be wonderful." Lila took a sip of her coffee. "I was thinking maybe I'd ask Brady what he's doing for New Year's Eve." She blushed at the thought of kissing him at midnight.

"I think that's a brilliant plan."

They finished their coffee while making plans—a few quiet days at the inn, then a trip to Denver where Sarah could show Lila her house, her school, and even where she grew up nearby in Broomfield.

"We should probably get downstairs for breakfast," Sarah said eventually. "Everyone else is probably in a hurry to get on the road today."

As they made their way to the lobby, Lila felt a mixture of excitement and nervousness about sharing their news. But looking at Sarah beside her, practically glowing with happiness, she knew they were making the right choice.

The dining room was quieter than usual when they arrived. Carol was setting up the breakfast buffet, but only six places were set at the table instead of the usual eight.

"It feels weird with Mike and Ali gone. Has anyone heard from her?" Lila asked.

Tom appeared from the kitchen with a fresh pot of coffee. "Ali called about an hour ago. Her sister had the baby.

It was a healthy little girl born at 11:57 p.m. on Christmas Day."

"Another Christmas baby," Brady said, looking up from where he was folding napkins. His eyes met Lila's across the room, and her chest fluttered.

"How wonderful," Sarah said softly. "I'm sure they're thrilled."

"Lila," Carol said, "Ali said to make sure and tell you she wrapped the baby's gift in birthday paper and not Christmas paper.

"I'm glad I was here to train her right," Lila joked.

The remaining guests filtered in as Carol finished setting out breakfast. Sophie and Miles looked rested and content, while Kimberly and Kendall seemed subdued at the prospect of leaving. Everyone filled their plates and settled around the table, the conversation quieter and more reflective than usual.

"I can't believe it's time to go home already," Kendall said, pushing her scrambled eggs around on her plate. "This week has gone by so fast."

"It really has," Sophie agreed. "Miles and I were just saying this morning how this has been one of our most memorable Christmases ever."

"Mine too," Kimberly said, glancing around the table. "I know we just met a week ago, but I feel like we're all family now."

Lila caught Sarah's eye across the table, and they shared a look of perfect understanding. This was their moment.

"Actually," Lila said, her heart beginning to race, "I have something I'd like to share with all of you."

The conversation stilled as everyone turned their attention to her. Brady set down his coffee mug and gave her an encouraging nod.

"You all know why I came to Pine Ridge," Lila continued. "I was looking for answers about my birth mother after discovering my baby quilt was made here by Emily."

"Have you learned anything new?" Miles asked gently.

Lila looked at Sarah, who reached over and took her hand. "We found each other," Sarah said, her voice thick with emotion.

The table went completely quiet for a moment as everyone processed what they'd just heard. Then Sophie gasped, her hand flying to her mouth.

"Sarah?" she whispered. "You're Lila's mother?"

Sarah nodded, tears streaming down her cheeks. "I am. I've been coming back to Pine Ridge every Christmas for thirty-four years because this is where she was born. I never dreamed that one day she'd find her way back here too."

The explosion of emotion that followed was loud and joyous. Kimberly burst into tears, Kendall jumped up to hug them both, and Miles had to wipe his eyes with his napkin. Even Tom looked misty-eyed as he watched the scene unfold.

"That's why you two seemed so connected from the very beginning," Sophie said, tears in her own eyes. "There was something there that none of us could quite put our finger on."

"The way you took care of each other," Kendall added. "It was like you already knew each other."

"In a way, we did," Sarah said, squeezing Lila's hand. "Sometimes there's an invisible string that connects you for reasons you don't know or understand at first."

Brady had remained quietly supportive throughout the revelation, but now he spoke up. "I've watched Sarah come here every Christmas for nearly twenty years," he said. "I always wondered what brought her back, what made this place so special to her. Now it all makes sense."

"It does," Carol said, wiping at her eyes. "Sarah, honey, I'm so happy for you. For both of you. To think that all these years, you were coming back to be close to her, and now you've found each other."

"It's a true Christmas miracle," Tom said, his deep voice gentle.

The breakfast that followed was filled with questions and stories and tears of joy. Sarah shared the story of Lila's birth, how she'd gone into labor during the Christmas Eve snowstorm. Carol chimed in with what she remembered. They both focused on the miracle of Lila's birth and not the difficult choices that came after.

"So, what happens now?" Kimberly asked as they finished eating. "Are you both leaving today?"

"Actually," Lila said, glancing at Sarah, "we're going to stay in Pine Ridge for a few more days. Just the two of us. We have thirty-four years to catch up on."

"And then Lila's going to come visit me in Denver," Sarah added. "I want to show her where I live, introduce her to my friends."

"That sounds perfect," Sophie said warmly. "What a way to start the New Year."

As the meal wound down and people began heading upstairs to pack, the mood grew bittersweet. These strangers who'd become family over the course of a week were about to scatter back to their regular lives.

"We have to stay in touch," Kimberly said, pulling out her phone. "All of us. I want to know how things go with you two." She glanced between Lila and Brady and wiggled her eyebrows. "And with you two as well."

The next hour was filled with tearful goodbyes. Sophie and Miles were the first to leave, promising to send photos from their next adventure. The sisters lingered longer, neither ready to go back to their normal lives.

"This isn't goodbye," Kimberly said fiercely as she hugged Lila and Sarah together. "We're family now. Real family. And families stay in touch."

"Always," Kendall agreed, wiping at her eyes. "And if you don't invite us to your wedding, I'll never forgive you." She looked pointedly at Brady.

Lila laughed despite her tears, glancing at Brady, who was helping Tom load luggage into cars. "I think you might be getting ahead of yourself."

"I don't think so," Kendall said with a knowing smile. "I've seen the way that man looks at you. Trust me on this one."

When the last car disappeared down the snowy driveway, Lila felt both empty and full at the same time. The inn seemed enormous with just the five of them—her and Sarah, Brady, Carol, and Tom.

"Well," Carol said, surveying the quiet lobby, "it's always strange when everyone leaves. The inn feels so big and empty."

"Not empty," Sarah said, settling into one of the chairs by the fireplace. "This place is always full of memories and love."

They spent the afternoon in comfortable quiet. Tom and Brady worked on some maintenance projects that had been put off during the busy holiday week. Carol caught up on paperwork in the office. Lila and Sarah sat by the fire, sometimes talking, sometimes just being together.

As evening approached, Brady found Lila in the lobby where she was curled up in a chair reading one of the books from the inn's small library.

"Want to take a walk?" he asked. "The snow's stopped, and it's beautiful out there."

They bundled up and stepped out into the crisp evening air. The world was pristine and white, the only sounds their footsteps and the distant call of a winter bird. They walked slowly along the sidewalk into town, neither in any hurry to reach a destination.

"How are you feeling?" Brady asked as they paused to look back at the inn, its windows glowing warmly in the gathering dusk.

"Like everything in my life has shifted," Lila said honestly. "A week ago, I was alone in the world, planning to spend Christmas by myself. Now I've had the most amazing and unexpected holiday ever. I have Sarah, and this place, and you." She looked up at him. "Especially you."

"Speaking of spending holidays alone, what are your plans for New Year's?" He grinned at her as he grabbed her hand and turned her toward him.

"Well, I asked Carol, and it sounds like my room is available on New Year's Eve. I thought maybe I'd come back from Denver and spend it with you. I'm very superstitious about the whole kissing someone at midnight thing."

"I say we practice, just to make sure we don't mess it up when it's the real thing."

She smiled up at him and nodded. "Yes, you know I like to be prepared."

"Ten, nine, eight, seven, six, five, four . . ." he began.

". . . three, two, one," she finished as he cupped her face in his gloved hands and leaned down to kiss her. His lips were full and warm, and it felt like coming home. Right here, in Brady's arms, is exactly where she belonged. She could feel it in her bones.

Kissing Brady, soft and sweet under the starry Colorado sky, Lila felt all the scattered pieces of her life clicking into place. She'd found so much more than she'd come here for, even more than she could have ever dreamed.

Behind them, the inn glowed with warm light, Sarah and Carol and Tom inside preparing dinner for their smaller group.

As they walked back toward the inn hand in hand, Lila realized that sometimes the most important journeys weren't about going somewhere new, but about finding your way back to where it all began. It was, she thought as they climbed the porch steps together, the perfect Christmas miracle.

Epilogue

One Year Later

Lila stood in the kitchen of Pine Ridge Inn rolling out dough to make cinnamon rolls for the next morning's breakfast. Through the window, snow was falling as Christmas lights on Brady's cabin twinkled in the distance.

A year ago, she'd been a hospitality consultant living in a sterile condo in California searching for a mother she'd never known. Now she was helping Brady run the Pine Ridge Inn, using her expertise to help him modernize their operations while preserving everything that made it special and unique.

Of course, they still debated about what needed to be updated, but he'd let her buy the Brew Pro 11 and even called his latte this morning, "Not half bad." It was progress.

"How are those coming along?" Brady asked, appearing behind her to wrap his arms around her waist and press a kiss to her temple.

"Almost ready for the morning," she said, leaning back against his warmth. "I still can't believe how much I love doing this."

"Even the early mornings?"

"Even the early mornings." She turned in his arms to face him. "Though I have to admit, knowing I get to see you makes getting up a lot easier."

Tom and Carol had officially retired, leaving Brady in charge. They still lived on the property and helped out, but it was more out of habit than obligation. They both loved meeting all the guests and having time to spend with them while Lila and Brady tended to the chores.

Lila had landed and successfully completed the job in Breckenridge. She had a new one starting after the New Year in Colorado Springs for a month, but she'd been living in her old room, the Pinecone Room, between assignments so she could help Brady at the inn.

The front door chimed with the arrival of guests, and Lila could hear Carol's warm voice greeting someone in the lobby. Their holiday guests would be checking in that afternoon, and Lila couldn't help thinking the group could never be as great as last year's had been.

"I should go help Carol get everyone settled," Lila said, but Brady's arms tightened around her.

"She's got it handled. Why don't you finish up here and then come join us in the lobby? I think you'll want to meet our guests."

Something in his tone made her study his face. "Is it someone famous?" she guessed.

"Just finish the cinnamon rolls first," he said, pressing another kiss to her forehead before disappearing toward the lobby.

Ten minutes later, Lila wiped her hands on her apron and made her way to the front of the inn. She could hear voices and laughter from the lobby, more animated than usual for guests who'd just met each other.

She rounded the corner and froze.

Sophie and Miles were sitting on the couch by the fireplace, looking exactly the same as they had a year ago. Kimberly was standing by the Christmas tree; her hands pressed to her mouth as if trying to contain her excitement. Kendall was snapping photos with her phone.

"Surprise!" Sarah called from across the room, her face glowing with delight.

Lila stared in shock as the pieces clicked together. "What—how—" She spun around to look at Brady, who was leaning against the doorframe with the biggest smile she'd ever seen.

"You did this," she breathed.

"We all did," Brady said. "Sarah helped coordinate everyone's schedules, and Carol handled the fake reservations so you wouldn't suspect anything."

Before Lila could respond, the front door opened again and Ali walked in, her hand resting on a distinctly rounded belly beneath her winter coat. Mike followed behind her, carrying their luggage and grinning.

"Ali!" Lila rushed over to hug her carefully. "You're pregnant!"

"Due in March," Ali said, her eyes sparkling with tears. "I couldn't miss this. None of us could."

Lila looked around at the faces surrounding her—the people who'd become family that first week, who'd witnessed her breakdown and breakthrough, who'd celebrated when she found Sarah, and cheered when she decided to stay in Pine Ridge.

"I can't believe you're all here," she whispered, overwhelmed by emotion.

"We missed you," Sophie said, rising from the couch to envelope Lila in a warm hug. "All of us. We've kept in touch, but it's not the same as being together."

"Plus," Kimberly added with a mischievous grin, "Brady said he had something important he wanted to share with all of us."

Lila turned back to Brady. Had he wanted to tell them he was taking over Pine Ridge Inn? That was no secret, least of all from her. He moved to her side, and she got nervous. Was this going where she thought it was going?

"Lila," Brady began, his voice steady but his eyes bright with emotion, "a year ago, you came to Pine Ridge looking for your past. You found Sarah, but you also found the rest of us."

He reached into his pocket and dropped to one knee, producing a small velvet box that made Lila's breath catch in her throat.

"I was lost before you got here," he continued. "Going through the motions, taking care of this place and these people but not really living. You changed everything. You made me want to dream again, to plan for a future instead of just surviving day by day."

Lila's hands flew to her mouth as tears streamed down her cheeks. Around the room, she could see their little holiday family watching with joy and anticipation. Sophie and Miles were holding hands, the sisters were recording everything on their phones, Ali was crying happy tears while Mike rubbed her back, and Sarah was practically glowing with pride and love.

"I wanted to ask you this question surrounded by the people who watched the beginning of our love story," Brady said, opening the box to reveal a beautiful vintage ring with a solitaire diamond. "The family who's going to celebrate with us for years to come."

He took a shaky breath. "Lila McAllister, will you marry me?"

"Yes," she whispered, then louder, "Yes! Of course, yes!"

The room erupted in cheers and applause as Brady slipped the ring onto her finger and stood to kiss her. Lila felt surrounded by love—Brady's arms, their friends' joy, her birth mother getting to be part of a major moment in her life, and the warm glow of the inn that had brought them all together.

"I love you," she whispered against Brady's lips.

"I love you too," he whispered back. "Welcome to the family, officially."

As they were swept up in hugs and congratulations, Lila caught Sarah's eye across the room. Her birth mother was crying openly; her hands pressed to her heart.

"I can't believe I get to see my daughter get engaged," Sarah said when Lila reached her. "I missed so many milestones, but I get to be here for this one."

"You'll be here for all of them from now on," Lila promised, hugging her tightly. "All the important ones and all the ordinary ones, too."

The rest of the evening passed in a blur of celebration and catching up. They gathered around the dining room table for dinner, sharing stories about the year that had passed. Sophie and Miles had gone on a cruise through the Greek isles and spent a month in Paris. The sisters had both gotten promotions at work and were planning a girls' trip to Europe in the spring, which Sophie and Miles were now helping them plan. Ali and Mike had bought their first house in Miami and were beside themselves with excitement about the baby.

"What about you?" Kendall asked Sarah. "Are you still in Denver?"

Sarah smiled, glancing at Lila. "Actually, I moved to Pine Ridge three months ago. There was an opening for an elementary school counselor, and I couldn't pass up the chance to be close to my daughter."

"And she's been helping us with the inn," Carol added from where she sat beside Tom. "Sarah's wonderful with the children of guests who visit. She has such a gift with kids."

"I love my work," Sarah said. "But I love being able to walk down the street to have coffee with Lila even more."

As the night wound down and everyone began heading to their rooms, Brady pulled Lila aside.

"Thank you," she said, touching the ring on her finger. "This was perfect. Having everyone here, doing it this way . . . it was everything I didn't even know I wanted."

"I wanted them all to be part of our story," Brady said. "They're the ones who saw the unlikely adventure that started that first day over coffee machine suggestions."

Lila laughed. "You were so stubborn about that coffee machine. I can't believe you took it to your cabin instead of letting it just die in peace."

"It makes perfectly good coffee."

"Brady Hanson, that machine is held together with duct tape and prayers."

"But still working." He grinned and pulled her closer. "Though I have to admit, your suggestion about the buffet setup was pretty smart."

"Only took you a year to admit it."

They stood quietly for a moment, looking around the lobby that had become the center of their world. The fire crackled softly, the Christmas tree sparkled with lights, and upstairs they could hear everyone settling in for the night.

"Do you ever think about that first day?" Brady asked. "When you walked in here looking lost and trying so hard to help everyone?"

"I wasn't lost," Lila protested. "I was being helpful."

"You were lost," he said gently. "We both were. But we found each other, and we found all of this." He gestured around the room. "Sometimes I think this place has magic in it."

"I know it does," Lila said. "Look what it gave us."

Christmas morning dawned clear and bright, with fresh snow sparkling on the mountains surrounding Pine Ridge. Lila woke early, as had become her habit, but instead of rushing to the kitchen, she lay quietly for a few moments.

A year ago, she'd woken up alone in this same room, anxious about confronting Carol with her suspicions. Now she woke up engaged to the love of her life, surrounded by family, in the place she'd never known she was looking for.

By the time they made it downstairs, Sarah was already in the kitchen, coffee made and breakfast preparations underway. She hummed as she worked, the same contentment radiating from her that Lila felt every day now.

"Need help?" Lila asked, tying on an apron.

"Always." Sarah smiled.

They worked side by side, the easy rhythm they'd developed over months of shared mornings. Through the kitchen windows, they could see their guests beginning to stir, lights coming on in windows throughout the inn.

"Are you happy?" Sarah asked quietly as they arranged fresh fruit on platters.

"Happier than I ever thought possible," Lila said honestly. "Are you?"

Sarah's smile was radiant. "I spent thirty-four years wondering if I'd made the right choice, wondering if you were okay, wondering if you were loved. Now I get to see every day that you're not just okay, you're thriving. You found exactly the life you were meant to have."

"We both did."

The morning that followed was filled with the kind of joy Lila had only dreamed of the year before. Their little family gathered around the breakfast table, sharing stories and laughter. Ali announced they were having a girl and had decided to name her Holly, in honor of the Christmas that had brought them all together. The sisters presented everyone with matching ornaments they'd had made, each one engraved with "Pine Ridge Family Christmas 2026."

After breakfast, they gathered around the Christmas tree for the traditional gift exchange. Brady surprised everyone with photos of their group from the year before, framed and ready to hang. Sarah gave Lila a scrapbook she'd been working on all year, filled with photos and mementos from their growing relationship.

"Look at this one," Kimberly said, holding up one of the photos. "It's from that first night at dinner. Look how Brady's trying not to look at Lila, and Lila's trying not to look at Brady, and meanwhile Sarah's sitting right between them like she knew exactly what was happening."

"I did know," Sarah said with a laugh. "A mother's intuition works even when she doesn't know she's a mother yet."

As the day wound toward evening, Lila found herself standing at the lobby windows, looking out at Main Street where the Christmas lights twinkled in the gathering dusk. The town looked exactly as it had the first time she'd seen it, but everything else had changed.

Brady appeared beside her, slipping his arm around her waist. "What are you thinking about?"

"Just . . . all of it. How different everything is from last year. How I came here thinking I was looking for one person, and instead I found everyone I needed."

"Any regrets?"

Lila looked around the lobby at their family—Sophie and Miles playing cards by the fire, the sisters fighting over which movie to watch, Sarah reading, and Tom and Carol looking through albums they kept from past Christmas groups. Through the dining room doorway, she could see the place settings already laid for dinner, the Christmas tree sparkling with lights and memories.

"None," she said, turning to face the man who'd become her home. "Not a single one."

"Good," Brady said, leaning down to kiss her forehead. "Because this is just the beginning."

Outside, snow began to fall on Pine Ridge once again, blanketing the town with the same magic that had brought them all together. But inside the inn, surrounded by love and laughter and the promise of all the Christmases to come, Lila had never felt more at home.

She'd come to Pine Ridge looking for her past and found her future instead. And as she watched their chosen family celebrate another Christmas together, she knew that sometimes the best journeys were the ones where you didn't know what lay ahead.

Hello, dear reader!

Thank you so much for picking up *Christmas at Pine Ridge Inn.* I hope you enjoyed being whisked away on a mental vacation to beautiful Pine Ridge!

If you'd like to know when my next book is out—and get access to bonus scenes and other freebies!—sign up for my newsletter below:

https://savannahcarlisle.com/newsletter

I won't share your information with anyone else! If you did enjoy *Christmas at Pine Ridge Inn*, I'd be so thankful if you'd write a review online. Getting feedback from readers helps to persuade others to pick up my book for the first time. It's one of the biggest gifts you could give me.

Want a free read? Check out a preview of my novella, *Finding You, Finding Me*, on the following pages.

Thanks again,
Savannah

Christmas Sugar Cookies

Ingredients (yields about 24 cookies):
2 ¼ cups all-purpose flour
½ teaspoon baking powder
¼ teaspoon salt
¾ cup (12 Tbsp) softened unsalted butter
¾ cup granulated sugar
1 large egg
2 tsp vanilla extract
¼ tsp almond extract (optional, but lovely)

Instructions:
Whisk together the flour, baking powder, and salt; set aside.

Cream butter and sugar until light and fluffy. Beat in egg, vanilla, (and almond extract if using).

Stir in the dry ingredients until just combined.

Divide the dough in half, roll each to about ¼-inch thickness (on parchment or silicone).

Chill the rolled dough for at least 2 hours (or up to 2 days).

Preheat oven to 350 °F.

Cut into shapes with cookie cutters, place on lined baking sheets about 3 in apart.

Bake 11–12 minutes (edges lightly tinged), let rest 5 minutes on pan, then cool fully on a rack.

When cool, decorate as you like (icing, glaze, buttercream, sprinkles) and enjoy!

Acknowledgements

Dear reader, thank you for reading Lila and Brady's story! I hope it took you on a mental vacation to somewhere that felt like snuggling up in a big, cozy blanket in front of a fireplace with a steaming mug of hot chocolate.

I'm a Hallmark Christmas movie junkie, and I've written about these movies for years for outlets like AARP and POPSUGAR. I came up with the idea for this one while watching Hallmark last year, and I knew it was time to write my first Christmas novel. I loved dreaming up the Pine Ridge Inn and all the friends we find there!

A big thank you to Olivia, my alpha reader who makes all my books better, and to my editor Lara Simpson, who polishes everything until it shines. For this one, I also got to work with the proofreader who's been marking up my writing since I first started stringing together sentences, my mother. No one loves a red pen like my mother!

I also have some of the best author friends a woman could ask for! Thank you to my author bestie Lindsay Gibson for always being just a text away, and to my Kiss Pitch 2022 group and the 2024 Debuts Discord for their continued advice, cheerleading and support.

Also to Kelsey, my author assistant, thank you for everything you do for me! When I get asked how I do as much as I do, I always say your name first. So grateful for you! (And readers, go check out Kelsey Whitney's books too!)

ARC team, you are amazing! Forget the Dallas Cowboys Cheerleaders...I have the best cheerleaders around! Every social media post, like, share, comment and DM means so much to me. I absolutely could not do this without you.

So many of my friends offer constant cheerleading and support through each and every one of my books. Shout out to Teresa, Maggie, Stephanie/Twinny, Michelle, Scarlett, Allyse, Noreen, Kristin and Zoe!

I also have the best family. Thank you to my parents, my brother Bo and his wife Nickki, and all my aunts, uncles and cousins for always believing in and encouraging me. I have some of the most amazing aunts: Shug, Luder Belle, Nank, Mary Ann and Judy. Also, Nancy, Gail and Vicky, my bonus aunts!

Shout out to all the sweet little girls in my life who love to see their names in my books: Azylinn, Ophelia, Maddy, Julie, Caroline, Maddie, Elaina, Finley, Poppy, Courtney, Montana, Chelsea and June!

I also married into the best family! Jane, Scott, Tonya, James and Julie—I'm so lucky to have all of you!

To my husband Chadd, happy "It's just another Thursday."

And, last but certainly not least, to my readers and reviewers. I appreciate every email, social post and review. I mean this from the bottom of my heart: I couldn't do what I love without you!

Want to Grab a Free Read?

Here's a sample of *Finding Me, Finding You*, a novella you can download for free now by joining my newsletter community!

"Need a little help there?"

The low, familiar timbre froze Rebecca St. Clair as she heaved her five-foot-five frame against her late Aunt Rhonda's front door. Seventeen years melted away in an instant as that voice—the one that had whispered in her ear on so many warm summer nights—washed over her like a wave from the nearby ocean.

Graham Nash.

She slowly turned to see him, wishing she'd taken the time to at least glance in the mirror when she'd washed her hands in the airport bathroom. No doubt, her long brunette hair was escaping her haphazard bun, and her mascara was smudged under her eyes from the tears that had escaped on her way into town.

He looked like he'd stepped straight out of a Hallmark movie. The casually handsome guy next door in his dark wash jeans and a gray t-shirt. His hands were stuffed in his pockets, an easy smile on his full lips.

"You have to turn the key to the right while you open the door handle." He nodded toward the lock where the key was still inserted.

Rebecca turned away from him, hoping the darkness that shrouded the front porch hid the bags under her eyes, and did as he instructed. The door popped open, because, of course, it did.

"Now I can check off saving a damsel in distress from my to-do list," he said from behind her.

He was clearly amused with the situation, but she didn't find it amusing at all. It had taken two flights, a lost rental car reservation, and an hour's drive from the Savannah airport to get to Sunrise Harbor. To her happy place.

Or at least, it had been her happy place a long time ago.

Stepping over the threshold with her carry-on suitcase, she took a deep breath before she turned to where he still stood on the porch. "Thank you. I didn't know you were back."

"Yep," he said, shifting his weight from one foot to the other. "Rhonda didn't tell you?"

Rebecca shook her head. "No." She didn't add that she hadn't spoken to her aunt for nearly a month before her sudden death from a brain aneurysm. Tears stung her eyes again like they had at the sight of the Sunrise Harbor sign on the way into the small Georgia beach town.

Aunt Rhonda's will had been delivered by her attorney to Rebecca's apartment with strict instructions not to have a funeral but instead to gather her closest friends one evening to celebrate her life. So, here she was, although she hadn't yet figured out how to get in the mood to celebrate.

Graham started to open his mouth again, but she cut him off. "Is there any chance we can reschedule this reunion for a later date? I'm sorry, but I can barely process why I'm here. I don't think I'm ready to revisit anything else yet."

Graham nodded, his gray eyes conveying that he understood. "You know where to find me." With that, he turned and bounded down the stairs to the sidewalk and disappeared into the night, presumably back to his parents' house next door.

Shutting the door behind her, Rebecca flipped on the light in the foyer and left her suitcase behind before moving into the living room. Sky blue and aqua pillows accented a beige sectional, and a giant piece of driftwood rose from the distressed wood coffee table in the middle of the room. The bookcases that flanked the flat-screen television were filled with books. She knew if she walked over they would range from the classics, like Jane Austen and F. Scott Fitzgerald, to the latest thrillers and rom-coms. Aunt Rhonda loved books, and she didn't discriminate against any genre or author.

The only thing you wouldn't find on these shelves was a Rhonda St. Clair book. That was because she only kept copies of her own books in her office. She thought it was too braggadocios to put the couple dozen books she'd authored in the living room where she entertained company.

Rebecca averted her eyes before they landed on the spot Aunt Rhonda had once told her she reserved for her only niece's future books. Rebecca had stood there with her as Aunt Rhonda had placed a decorative vase of silky blue hydrangeas in the spot, saying, *"We'll put a placeholder here until I can shelve your books right alongside the greats and tell all my friends about my famous niece the author."*

She knew without looking the vase was still there. Another reminder of things lost.

Going to sit at the seagrass barstools that faced into the kitchen, Rebecca pulled her phone out of her pocket and dialed her mother.

"How was the drive?" she asked Rebecca after they exchanged greetings.

"Fine. I forgot how dark it is on her street. I almost missed the driveway."

"It's sea turtle season," her mother said by way of explanation. Streetlights and house lights had to be off or replaced with amber, orange, or red bulbs during the nesting season from March through October to prevent baby turtles from heading toward the road when they hatched instead of the ocean.

"Yeah, I forgot. In the city, you avoid unlit streets."

"As you should," her mother said, the worry present in her voice like any time they talked about Rebecca living in Manhattan. It didn't matter she'd lived there nearly for twenty years. Her mother was still convinced she'd get robbed, kidnapped, or murdered every time she stepped out of her apartment building.

"Is everything in the house okay?" she asked Rebecca.

Aunt Rhonda had been Rebecca's late father's only sister, and they'd fallen out of touch after his death when her mother got remarried.

"I just got in, but everything seems fine. Stella stopped by to clean things up and make sure a room was ready for me," she said, referring to her Aunt Rhonda's best friend Stella. "She's coming by tomorrow to talk me through what I need to do to sell it."

"Honey, are you sure that's what you want to do? You always loved Aunt Rhonda's house. She left it to you for a reason."

Rebecca felt a pang of guilt that she'd only returned to town to say goodbye to the house one last time. Aunt Rhonda had never given her any conditions or voiced any expectations when it came to her plan to leave Rebecca the house. It had simply always been the plan since she had no children of her own. But the guilt was there just the same.

"I never have time to come down here, and the town regulations don't allow rentals in this area. It doesn't make sense for it to sit here empty. Besides, the taxes and insurance would completely blow my budget."

Her mother sighed, and she already knew what she was going to say before she said it.

"But you could live there for free. The house is paid for. Maybe you could even start writing again."

Rebecca was shaking her head before she finished. "My life is in New York, Mom. I can't just quit my job and lie on the beach and write. I still have to make money to pay my bills and feed myself. Besides, I barely even know anyone here."

Graham's angular face and perfectly symmetrical dimples flashed through her mind. He had dark stubble where his face had once been smooth as a teenager. Graham, she knew all too well.

"Promise me you'll think about it," came her mother's soothing tone on the other end of the line. "You have two weeks there. No need to rush the decision."

Rebecca sighed. "I promise." She said it to appease her mother because she'd already made the only rational decision. She'd sell the house and pay off the rest of her student loans. There might even be a little left over to put into her nearly nonexistent savings account.

When she ended the call with her mother, she noticed a new text from her boss, Chet Tanner.

Chet Tanner

> *Did you see my email? I need the pro forma on Ryland Towers before my 9 a.m. tomorrow.*

She'd promised Chet she'd work on her "vacation." She was the CFO for a large real estate company, which touted its flexible hours and unlimited vacation time while regularly working her twelve-plus hours a day and expecting her to be available 24/7, 365 days a year.

She wanted to say something passive-aggressive like, *Per my email this morning, I arrived at my aunt's house at 9 p.m. and plan to work into the night to ensure you have it by 8 a.m. to review before your meeting.*

Rebecca had never missed a deadline in two years of working for Chet, and yet, he still felt the need to micromanage her with dozens of emails and texts a day asking for updates on projects that weren't due yet. He'd been the first person to offer her a C-suite role though, and it paid well. She knew it was a classic golden handcuffs situation, but Manhattan was an expensive place to live and she'd had to take out loans for her joint Master of Accountancy and MBA program.

The recruiter she'd been working with to find a new CFO role told her to hang in a little longer until he could find her the right role. She couldn't risk leaving and having a gap on her resume to explain.

Her jaw clenched as she typed out a more appropriate reply to Chet.

Rebecca St. Clair

I've made it safely to my destination and will have it in your inbox by 8 a.m. so you can review it before your meeting.

After shoving her phone in her back pocket, Rebecca collected her suitcase from the foyer and made her way to the guest bedroom that had always been hers as a girl. She'd spent a month every summer in Sunrise Harbor, and when she left, she'd count down the days until she returned on a big wall calendar back on her bedroom wall in the suburbs of Raleigh.

Turning on the overhead light, she stopped in the doorway to take it all in. The double bed still had the same blue and white quilt her grandmother had made when she was a child with pillow shams to match. The little desk where she'd sat to write was still positioned under the window with a view of the beach over the dunes that protected the cottage from high tides and storms.

On the wall with the closet was the familiar white-washed bookcase filled with books. *The Babysitters Club*, Beverly Cleary's *Ramona Quimby* collection, *Choose Your Own Adventure*, *Goosebumps*, and her aunt's complete *Nancy Drew* collection. They were all there.

As she turned around in the room again, taking it all in, tears filled her eyes. Everything was exactly the same.

And yet, nothing would ever be the same again.

Keep reading for free at https://savannahcarlisle.co m/fmfy

Preview More by Savannah Carlisle

The Library of Second Chances

Bookstore owner Lucy Sullivan is a third-generation resident of tiny Heron Island, and she's tired of outsiders coming in and destroying their small-town charm in the name of progress. The town wasn't enough for her mother—or more recently, her ex-fiancé—but it's been the one constant in her life, and she's not going to sit by while it's destroyed.

Logan Lancaster was brought in to find a profitable solution to the town's failing budget. Lucy is a worthy opponent, and he knows he can help both the town and her struggling bookstore if only she wasn't so stubborn. He can't make the mistake of mixing business and pleasure again though. After all, choosing love over business had blown up in his face back in San Diego, and this is his last chance to salvage his career.

Unbeknownst to them, they're falling in love through anonymous notes exchanged in books left in the town's Little Free Library as *Island Girl* and *Gatsby's Ghost*.

As they spar over the town's waterfront, Logan helps Lucy with some ambitious plans for her bookstore. Their connection grows, but Logan must grapple with whether to reveal his true identity to *Island Girl* when he uncovers the truth or leave as planned. Lucy, fearing abandonment, faces the biggest risk of her life—trusting that love will make Logan stay.

Will Logan choose love over ambition, or will their secrets tear them apart? Find out in this heartfelt contemporary romance, where a Little Free Library holds the key to love and the courage to take a chance.

Read Now: https://geni.us/tlsc

The Summer of Starting Over

Thirteen years ago, Callie Jackson left Big Dune Island with nothing but her guitar and dreams of country music stardom. She found success beyond her wildest imagination—until her empire came crashing down in a storm of betrayal and financial fraud.

Now she's forced to return home to clean out her family's historic beach house, the last thing she wants to do. But when she arrives, she finds more than just memories waiting for her. Jesse Thomas—the boy she left behind to chase her dreams—is renovating the very house she's come to sell.

As Callie rediscovers her musical roots at the town's beloved Beach Bash festival where she was first discovered, she realizes that somewhere between the glossy pop productions and stadium tours, she lost her authentic voice.

And maybe, just maybe, the key to finding it again lies in the place—and the person—she left behind.

But Jesse has dreams of his own now, and they don't include reopening old wounds. As they're thrown together to save the festival that launched her career, Callie and Jesse must decide if they can build something new from the broken pieces of their past—or if some bridges, once burned, can never be rebuilt.

A heartfelt story about second chances, finding your true voice, and the courage it takes to let yourself fall in love with the same dream twice.

Read Now: https://geni.us/tsso

If I'd Have Known

A career-driven lawyer and ex-baseball player must save a historic B&B from developers while planning their friends' secret wedding—but there's a surprise in store they won't see coming.

As a successful lawyer in her island hometown, Georgia "Gigi" Franklin has her life perfectly arranged – until she's forced to work with former MLB star Austin Beckett. Planning their best friends' secret wedding means constant bickering that masks a growing attraction neither wants to acknowledge.

Gigi has spent her life rejecting her mother's traditional expectations, building walls around her heart in the name of independence. Austin understands – he's been running from his own family legacy in baseball. But when he starts coaching a local youth team and bonds with a young foster child named Luke, he begins to see family in a different light.

As they uncover the truth about an inheritance dispute at the beloved Salty Breeze B&B, Gigi and Austin discover they have more in common than they thought. Could planning the perfect wedding lead them to their own happily ever after? And could Luke be the key to healing not just their relationships with their parents, but also their hearts?

Romance blooms on Big Dune Island in this heartwarming story about family, second chances, and learning that love doesn't have to mean losing yourself.

Read Now: https://geni.us/iihk

About Savannah

Savannah Carlisle writes heartwarming romance novels with idyllic settings. Her stories transport readers to fun and quirky small towns where friends feel like family.

In her other life, Savannah's name is Kristi Dosh, and she writes about something completely different: the business of college sports. She has written for such outlets as Forbes, ESPN, Fast Company, Entrepreneur, *The Washington Post* and more.

Savannah/Kristi is a former practicing attorney who lives on Amelia Island with her husband, a German Shepherd and three cats.